시로 쓴 조선의 레전드

추사 김정희

Chusa Kim Jeong Hui

1

신익선

시로 쓴 조선의 레전드

추사 김정희 1

Chusa Kim Jeong Hui

인쇄일 | 2024년 6월 20일
발행일 | 2024년 6월 27일

지은이 | 신익선
펴낸이 | 설미선
펴낸곳 | 뉴매헌출판
출판등록 | 2018년 3월 30일
주소 | 충남 예산군 예산읍 교남길 33
E-mail | new-maeheon@hanmail.net

값 18,000원
ISBN 979-11-984692-7-4(03810)

시로 쓴 조선의 레전드

추사 김정희

Chusa Kim Jeong Hui

1

신익선

뉴 NEW
매헌
梅軒出版

　추사 김정희 선생 출생 시 조선의 내외정세는 이미 불꽃 튀는 격동기였다. 서구열강이 쉴 새 없이 개화의 깃발을 펄럭이는데도 오로지 왕만이 무소불위의 권력을 갖고 있던 때였다. 이른 봄철 산비둘기 울음 길동무 삼아 화전민으로 전락한 백성들이 귀엽고 예쁜 그들의 어린 것들을 생으로 굶겨 죽이고는 반실성하여 헛소리하다 뒤따라 죽기 예사인 시절이었다.

　그나마 제왕다운 풍모가 강하던 정조가 급서하자 국운이 쇠퇴 일변도로 기울기 시작했다. 나라를 움직이는 조정신료들은 당쟁에 급급한 나머지 국가의 근본인 백성들 살림살이를 걱정할 겨를이 없었다. 순조 등극 후부터 대왕대비가 수렴청정하는 조선왕조의 부귀는 온통 권신權臣들 차지였다. 왕실과 세도문중, 양반, 심지어 고을 아전들까지 합세하여 백성 고혈 빨아먹으면서도 소득 산업인 상업을 가장 천시하여 실질을 저버렸다. 반상班常이 극심한 양반사회에서 신분제도는 엄격하였고 형벌은 무거웠다. 사회지도층은 소득 없이 공리공론을 일삼아 하루도 끊일 날 없는 당쟁의 폐해로 날로 텅 빈 국고의 한숨이 퍼져나갔다.

　이 글은 당리당략에 치우쳐 변화와 개방, 개혁을 등한시하여 혼란하였던 조선후기를 시대상으로 하여 정치가와 예술인으로서 한 시대를 풍미하였던 추사를 주인공으로 쓴 시집이다. 예산에서 태어나 한양 월성위 문중을 이어받은 추사의 삶을 조망한 글이다. 운명이라 해야 하나? 추사는 스스로를 죄인이라 불렀지만 추사는 윤상도 상소와 관련이 없었다. 그 어떤 죄도 없었다. 죄가 있다면 세도정치였다. 추사를 고문하며 36대의 곤장을 친 형장과 제주도 위리안치 및 북청 유배는 당시 권력층의 몫이어야 옳다. 그러나 이는 끝내 혁파되지 않았다.

이 폐단의 지속은 결국 일제의 조선침략으로 귀결되었지만, 세도정치는 당대 조선국에서 이미 학예의 최고 경지에 이르렀던 추사에게 엄청난 불운이었다. 허나 불후의 업적인 세한도와 추사체 정립 등의 빛나는 예술세계는 아이러니하게도 그 불운이 모태가 되었다. 이 시집은 그러한 추사의 궤적만을 살펴 쓴 시집이다. 다음권에서 추사의 진면목에 해당하는 학문의 위대한 성취 및 추사체와 추사의 예술세계를 살펴 완결지을 것임을 밝힌다.

모쪼록 작은 이 시집이 불요불굴의 정신으로 시, 서, 화, 경학, 감상, 금석학, 고증학, 불교학의 새 역사를 개척한 추사 김정희 선생을 기리게 되길 빈다. 더하여 일대의 통유通儒, 우리 온 겨레의 혼불이신 추사 김정희 선생을 만나 뵙는 글이 되길 염원한다.

2024. 5.

산정 신익선 識

By the time Chusa was born, Joseon's domestic and foreign situations were in a fiery turbulent era. At that time, the royal command still had a overwhelmingly dominant power while Western Powers were waving the flags of the open door to enlightenment. Then in early spring, a number of people who were degraded to slash and burn farmers, traveling with the song of turtledoves, often starved their cute and lovely children to die shiftlessly and then went mad, yelling out things and followed them to the grave.

After King Jeongjo with kingly dignity died suddenly, Joseon slowly declined. Due to party strife, government officials had no time to worry about people's livelihood, the backbone of the nation. Since Queen Dowager's regency after Soonjo's accession to the throne, wealth had been in the clutch of powerful courtiers. Royal family, 'Sedo' clan, and Yangban combined by even petty officials sucked the blood of the people and lost practical interest, belittling the commerce, the income source. In Yangban society, a rigid caste system, caste system was strict and punishment was severe. While the government officials lapsed into empty formalities, the state coffers were depleted by the constant party strife as time went on.

These poems are for Chusa who lived as a politician and artist in one in late Joseon, when was in turmoil, putting party interests first and neglecting changes and an open door to reform. Through the poems, you can look into the life of Chusa who was born in Yesan and inherited Wolsungwee clan. Was it a fate? Chusa professed to be a criminal himself, but he was not involved in the appeal against Yoon Sangdo. He was innocent. if anything, Sedo politics were guilty. They deserved tortures, 36 beatings and the exile to Jeju island and Bukcheong which Chusa experienced. However, the government system was never reformed. These continuous evils resulted in the Japanese annexation of Korea, and Sedo politics were also such a disaster to Chusa. Nevertheless, it was ironical that his brilliant art world such as his immortal masterpiece, Sehando and Chusa's writing style was formed by his miserable life. Book one deals with the traces of Chusa's life. Book two covers his academic achievement, writing style, and art world.

Hopefully, the poetical works will pay a tribute to Chusa Kim Jeonghui who rewrote the history of poetry, calligraphy, ink painting, Chinese classics, appreciation, epigraphy, the study of ancient documents, and the Buddhist study with an invincible spirit. In addition, I hope you will meet Chusa Kim Jeonghui, a worldly-wise and executive scholar and the soul of the people in one.

2024. 5.

Sanjeong Shin Ik-seon

제2장 조선의 금강경

추사의 사행단 행보에서
대과급제까지

The Most Excellent Sutra of Joseon

From Diplomatic Mission to the Pass
of the State Examination

제4장 조선의 씨눈
추사의 제주도
유배에서 죽음까지

The Embryo of Joseon
Chusa's Exile to Jeju and Bukcheong
and His Death

서까래에 내린 초승달빛 품고 사는 예산 향저鄕邸시렁,

예산 구렁목 금강송 붉은 가지로 만든 도끼자루를 가진 손도끼 있다

붓을 물고 있는 얄팍한 대나무가 벼린 붓끝

옹골찬 도끼자루 결 따라 만나는 뭉툭한 도끼의 날처럼

저 바싹 날선 붓이 사정없이 정수리 내리치는 일순간의 그 찰나다

여섯 살 먹은 손으로 월성위 궁 대문에 쓴 입춘첩이

형조참판, 지금의 법무부차관을 포박, 주리 틀어

무려 엿새 동안 모진 고문을 하고 서른여섯 대의 태장을 안기다 못해

무려 만 구년 사 개월, 쉰다섯 살에서 예순여섯 해 동안

인두불로 지진 상처에 검붉은 피멍울 터트려 핀 새빨간 동백꽃잎 무색해라

황량한 제주와 북청 들판 울리는 대장간 쇠망치로

바로 눈앞에서 빤히 쳐다보며 번번이 칠흑의 죽음을 두드렸다

돌과 바람, 절망과 체념, 그리고 몽당붓들의 눈알인 추사체,

그 어떤 희망도 품을 수 없는 폐허의 골짜기에서

모든 걸 내려놓고서야 비로소 우주의 한 존재, 내자를 만나

오직 결기로 뭉쳐진 웅혼한 폐부에 소용돌이친 그를 보다

뼈아팠던 일생이었으나 도도한 자존, 시대를 초월한 해학으로

마침내 자화煮火하는 일흔한 살의 추사 몸짓에 섞여

승천, 동지 지나 하늘로 날아오르고 있다 포르릉 날렵하게 산새도 날아

반도의 중심 예산에서 온 겨레에게 추사라는 삶과 붓도끼 날다

On the rafters of the main home in Yesan that the crescent moon shines

There's a hatchet with a helve made of the red trunk of a Geumgang pine in Gooreungmok.

A forged brush tip stuck in a thin bamboo

Like the blade of a stubby axe which follows the grain,

The sharp brush is about to strike the head top without mercy.

Spring slips pasted on the gate of Wolsungwee which the child at 6 wrote

Resulted in tying up a vice-minister of Ministry of Justice to twist his legs,

To torture and give 36 beating for 6 days.

For as many as 9 years 4 months of fifty-five to sixty-six years

Red camellias pale by red bruises that the burns seared with a hot iron burst,

With the hammer with which the fields of Buckcheong and desolate Jeju rang

He stroke the pitch dark death repeatedly, staring at it right before him.

Stone and wind, despair and resignation, and Chusache, eyeballs of stubby brushes

In the hopeless valley of ruins,

It was not until he put down everything that he met self, Cosmic Being

And saw himself, all straight and strick, swirling in the sublime heart.

Life marked by suffering, yet lofty self-esteem and humor that transcended time

Mix with the gestures of Chusa at 71 who finally turned to Buddhism

And now fly up into the sky to ascend to heaven. So does a little bird.

The life and brush hatchet of Chusa fly to all people from Yesan, center of the peninsula

조선의 애기먼동

추사의 탄생에서 결혼까지

The Dawn of Joseon

From Chusa's Birth to Marriage

조선의 애기먼동

혼돈의 세기, 어둔 조선국 새벽에 홀로 고개 내미는 새벽별 아닌가
임진왜란과 병자호란의 두 번에 걸친 큰 병화에 시달리고도
국가개조의 혁신과 개방을 도외시하고 더더욱 부국강병을 멀리한 조선은
당쟁으로 숙종 조 갑술환국(1694년) 때 남인들이 대거 숙청되고
탕평책을 쓴 영조 때 왕실과 사림 간의 혼인으로 척족세도가 발호하다
출구 없는 극심한 당쟁으로 건국이념인 성리학은 허례로 전락,
남인계열 성리학자들은 실학, 곧 성리학의 '근본을 회복'하려 했고
재야 사림 역시 반성과 비판하기 이르렀으니 이가 곧 실학사상의 발이다
북학, 곧 청조清朝를 풍미하는 고증학풍을 중시한 이들이 북학파다
영조 때 홍대용, 박지원 등 사행단 자제들에 의하여 주창된 북학파는
사회개혁과 정치혁신을 도모하였으나 한직에 머물러 뜻을 이루지 못했다
이들 중에서 가장 열혈인물이 박제가다, 박제가의 제자가 추사다
광풍 먹고 자란 광기의 사내 초정의 품 안에서 막 떠오르는 추사야말로
새롭고도 신선한 기운 넘치는 조선 학예를 새로이 창건한
산이 예를 올리듯 둘러선 예산에서 떠오르는 조선의 애기먼동 아닌가

* 초정 : 박제가의 호

The Dawn of Joseon

The chaotic age, a morning star sticks its head alone out of Joseon's dark dawn

Even after ravaged by invasions from Japan and Manchuria

Joseon disregarded its reform and the open door, not to mention the its prosperity and defense

In 1694 during King Sukjong reign, the majority of Namin was purged

And in the reign of King Yeongjo who pursued the Tangpyeongchaek, Sedo politics by royal in-law family started

The ceaseless strife degraded Neo Confucianism, Joseon's founding principle into empty formalities.

On the contrary, Namin scholars strived to recover the root idea of Neo Confucianism, and

The scholars out of office also took time for introspection and criticism, which later became Practical Learning Thought

Bukak, Bukak school which highly regarded the historical research, a influential study of Qing China

The scholars such as Pak Jiwon and Hong Daeyong in the reign of Youngjo advocated Buhak.

Though planing a social reform and a political innovation, they failed to realize their aspiration because of their trivial positions.

Among them, Park Jega, Chusa's master, was most passionate.

A fanatical man that was nourished with wild winds. Just rising from Chojeong's bosom

Chusa, who made Joseon's arts and sciences fresh and vigorous anew, was

A rising dawn in Yesan surrounded by mountains, which looked as if to observe courtesy.

석정 石井

신암 추사고택 뒷산 용산의 외침소리,
아기의 출생을 알리는 외침이 퍼지는 유월 아침결
웬일로 남녘 불꽃바람 불어 새잎 시들고
사계절 우러나오던 달디단 우물
담장 밖 샘물이 돌연 흐름 멈추고 스스로 응고하다
그 새벽 청천, 푸른 하늘에 낙뢰 치다
비 오지 않는데 산 뒤덮는 초여름 무지개 타고
바람 일으키며 용龍오르는 구렁목 마을
저 삼태기 안 아늑한 동네에서 솟구쳐
조선국 추사의 탄생을 처음 태허太虛에 알리자마자
콸콸콸 다시 샘솟는 석정 눈시울의 숨소리들
모란꽃 흐드러진 언덕 산비둘기가
생애 첫 부리로 쪼아대는 짙푸른 음성에
삼천리 산천 화들짝 놀라 멈춘 샘물의 힘 터트리는
영혼물인가, 양수 터져 흐르는 어미 우물

* 석정 : 충남 예산군 신암면 용궁리 추사고택 두레박 샘의 이름.
* 태허 : 『장자』의 「지복유」에 처음 나오는 말로 우주의 큰 공간.

A Stone Well

The cry of Yongsan at the back of Chusa's old house in Sinam.

The cry of a newborn baby echoing around in June morning

The hot wind blowing from the South made the new leaves wither unexpectedly,

The well spouting great tasting water all year around,

The spring water outside of the fence abruptly stopped flowing and solidified itself

At the dawn, lightning struck through blue sky

And the early summer rainbow rose without rain, covering the hill

Onto it, a dragon flied up, creating winds from Gooreungmok Village

Bursting from the straw basket shaped village

On letting God know Chusa' birth

Tears' breath, the spring gushing glub, glub, glub again.

In the hill full of peony, at turtledoves'

Deep blue coo, pecking with the life first beak,

The whole land of Joseon was startled and the quiescent spring water spouted

Is it the water for the soul? The mother's well like her water broken.

탄생

꿈틀, 예산의 신암 마을 용산이 무릎 당겨
조심조심 기계유씨의 태중 아이 받아낸다
갓 스물한 살에 첫 자식, 추사를 얻는 경주 김씨 김노경이
땀에 전 지어미의 아미 쓸어내릴 때
흠칫, 대국이라 떠받들던 청나라가 크게 놀라다
추사, 오직 이 이름만으로 청나라를 제압하여
동양문화권의 주도국이란 누대에 걸친 중국의 자부심을 깨부수어
중국문화의 한반도 지배구조 구도가 무너진 그 해,
모차르트가 '피가로의 결혼'을 쓰다
조선 천주교 첫 순교자 정약종은 세례를 받다
무더운 기운이 초여름 대지를 감싸는 유월 새벽에
그윽하고 고요한 둥지의 신암고을 흔들리고
농가월령가를 쓴 정학유와 승려 의순을 낳은 그 해우년,
바로 병오년 유월 초사흘 인시 무렵이다
그날 이른 새벽부터 딱딱딱 딱따구리 징 쳐대자
구렁목 쩌렁 울리는 태아의 우렁찬 옥음,
훗날 학예의 새 세계를 개국할 해동옥음海東玉音 발하며
꿈틀, 마침내 조선 학예의 새 군주 탄생하다

* 용산 : 추사고택 뒤편에 있는 산 이름.
* 병오년(1786년) : 정조 10년, 청 고종 건륭 51년, 일 덴메이 천황 6년, 조선의 수도 한
  성부 인구 19만 명, 조선국 전국 총인구 733만 명.

22

Birth

A wriggle! Yongsan (the hill) of Sinam in Yesan pulled its knees
And delivered Gigae Yoo's fetus carefully.
When Kim Nogyeong from Gyeongju Kim Clans having his first child at 21
Wiped his wife's sweaty brow,
Started, greatly surprised was the Qing China highly respected as a big country
Only by repute, Chusa subdued the Qing,
In that year, when he hurt its pride that the oriental culture had
originated from China and
Its cultural domination over the Korean Peninsula collapsed,
Mozart wrote 'the Marriage of figaro' and
Jeong Yakjong, the first Korean Catholic martyr, was baptized.
On June dawn, when heat waves enveloped the earth,
The nest shaped Sinam village, calm and mellow, was shaken.
In that year when all anxiety was melted and Jeong Hakyoo, the
writer of the lyrics, Nongga Wollyeongga and Eu Soon, a buddhist
monk were born
Around 3 to 4 on June 4th in 1786
When the woodpecker kept knocking from early dawn,
The first cry of the baby filled the Gooreungmok shrilly and beautifully
Beautiful cry, which would open a new world of liberal arts
A wriggle. Finally, the King of Korean liberal art was born.

조부祖父, 너털웃음 웃다

아가야, 내 품에 안겨 쌔근쌔근 잠든 정희야
너 출생하고 이 할아비가 이제 대사헌이다
네가 탄생한 이후 우리 문중이 평온하고 번성하다
월성위궁 작은 모래 한 알, 미세한 바람 한 올이 신선하다
이 할아비가 새벽 미명에 가장 먼저 일어나
대청마루 안뜰 거니는 것을 너는 알아보느냐
할아빈 네가 있어 늘 기쁘고 신명난다
애야, 건강하게 성장하여 한몫 단단히 하여다오
네 백부와 네 아비가 대과급제하여 성총을 입었으니
대대로 이어져 오는 가훈인 직도이행直道以行,
너는 우리 문중의 선한 기풍을 밖에 크게 드날리라
천하가 너로 인하여 새봄이 되게 하라
무릇 나라의 문文이야말로 치세의 근본,
글을 가까이 하며 고요히 성현의 도를 궁구하라
새 학문 일으켜 정신을 맑게, 의지를 굳세게 다지면서
문중과 나라를 튼튼히 새롭게 하라
싱그러운 유월 초록 어깨 두드려 주려무나
잘 커서 잔칫상 펼치고 한 자리서 박장대소拍掌大笑하자
정희야, 이 할아비 웃음 들리느냐, 우리 아가야

* 직도이행直道以行 : '바른 도리로써 행하라' 라는 추사 가문의 가훈.

Grandfather's Hearty Laugh

Jeonghui, sleeping soundly in my arms, sweetie
After your birth, I, your granddad, became Inspector General
And your presence brought peace and prosperity to my family.
Even a grain of sand and gentle breeze in Wolsungwee Palace are fresh.
You know I got up first before dawn and
Walked around in the yard of the hall?
You make me exalted and exhilarated.
Sweetie, grow well and be an asset to the country
Because your uncle and father passing the state exam received a royal grace.
With our family motto, '直道以行' that means 'do right'
Raise our family ethos widely.
You should be a person bringing new spring to the world
Know that liberal arts are the basics of peaceful ruling
With your mind refreshed and your purpose hardened, open new study.
Make both our family and the country new and strong.
Tap June on the fresh green shoulder
Grow well and giving a party, let's laugh aloud clapping our hands
in the future.
Jeonghui, can you hear me laughing, my sweetie?

* Jeonghui : Chusa's realname

오석산 참나무꽃
- 추사 어머니 기계유씨의 독백

불러라 언제 어디서건 나를 불러라
목울대 터지도록 언제 어디서든 나를 불러라
이 향기로운 유월 신록의 푸름에
온몸 쩍쩍 갈라진 벌거숭이로 나는
억새밭 띠 헤집으며 네 이름에 들테나
네 콧물과 네 한숨과 네 환희와
네 살과 네 뼈와 네 찬란한 혼백 보듬고
내 몸 산산이 찢어 하늬바람 피워
내가 믿고 의지하는 너
설한풍 이겨내고 다시 잣는 나의 물레인 너
너 태어나고 내가 묻힐 땅에 피어
겹겹이 둘러쳐진 꽃잎 칭칭 동여매고
발그스레한 심경心經의 붉은 피로
희미한 별빛 깨워 동트는 새벽 미명의 너는
너는 나의 젖꼭지, 오석산 참나무 꽃

* 오석산 : 예산 신암면에 위치한 해발 97m 높이의 화암사 뒤편의 산 이름.
* 심경 : 반야바라밀다심경의 준말.

The Oak Flowers in Oseoksan

- Mother's Monologue

Call me anytime and anywhere.

Call me anytime and anywhere screaming at the top of your lungs.

In the fresh verdure of fragrant June

I, naked splinted all over the body

Will go into you, cleaving a way through silver grass field.

Embracing your nasal mucus, your sign, your joy,

Your bone and flesh, and your glorious soul

I, with my body torn into pieces, will make a west wind

You, who I believe in and depend on

You, my spinning wheel turning again after overcoming the cold winter

In the ground where you were born and I will be buried

Will grow and bloom with layers of petals.

With the red blood of rosy Prajna-paramita Sutra

You, break of day which wakes a dim starlight

Are my nipple, and oak flowers in Oseoksan.

추사의 장작불

아기의 첫 울음소리는 아궁이 가득 지피는 장작불

불이웃집 농부들 놀라 새벽부터 텃밭 두둑에 허리 굽혀
골골마다 씨앗이랑 세워간다
옆집 선비는 책상머리 새벽 글 읽기 시작하고
빈 둥지 남겨놓고 떠난 산새들은 산봉우리를,
학자는 진중한 학문의 글 이랑을,
수처작주입처개진隨處作主入處開眞, 진리는 깨달음을
만물은 각기 제 처소에서 각자의 소리로 지피는 불,

억겁 달려온 아승지겁의 숨 가쁜 울음소린,
아기의 저 울음소린 어린 추사가 아궁이에 불 지피는 화목,
가열하게 불 지펴 화부가 피워내는 저것은

불길의, 붓의, 불꽃의, 번갯불의, 추사의 장작불 아닌가

* 수처작주입처개진 : 중국의 고승 임제대사가 쓴 『임제록』에서 따온 말. 직역을 하면,
'수처隨處, 곧 현재 있는 곳에 따라서 주인이 되라. 그러면 서있는 곳 모두가 참된 것
이다.'란 뜻.
* 아승지겁阿僧祇劫: 어떤 시간의 단위로도 측정할 수 없는 무한히 긴 시간.

Wood Fire

A baby first cry was a burning wood fire crammed in the furnace

Rudely awakened by the cry, neighbor's farmers stoop down from dawn,
Plough furrows and plant the seedlings,
And neighbor's scholar starts to read a book.
The birds leaving its nest dream about the mountaintop, and
The scholars the furrow in writing of serious study.
'If the independent person does his best now and here, all of thing
will be true!'. The truth kindles the fire of enlightenment, and
All things in place with their voice light a fire.

The breathless cry taking eternity,
The baby's cry was firewood with which little Chusa made a fire in
the fireplace
The fire a stoker built

Was a brush, flare, flame, lightning, and Chusa's wood fire!

월성위궁 백송의 묵음

서산 대교리에서 살다가 이사와 정착한 예산 신암,
서기 어린 뜰 드넓은 평야 이루는데다 기름지다

순전히 농사를 위하여 팔봉산 턱에 터 잡은
속칭 '한다리 김문金門'으로 불린 추사의 고조는 김흥경이다
신암땅, 비산비야의 터전에서 벼슬이 영의정에 닿고
아들 김한신이 영조의 부마, 월성위에 봉하여지자
영조대왕은 딸과 사위를 위하어 월성위궁,
현재의 서울 통의동 백송나무골 저택을 하사하다

조선에서 유일하게 듣는 백송의 청청한 묵음,
예산의 흰 소나무가 꿈꾸며 머지않아 만나게 될
시대를 채근하여 미래에 학예의 새 시대 열어갈 흰 싹
향리인 신암 용궁리 사전賜田에 심은 백송이다

월성위궁 백송에서 훗날 용궁리 백송, 이 백송이
후손인 추사의 몸이자 정신, 꼿꼿한 추사가 저 백송이라

싹둑 잘린 절정에서 밀어 올리는 우듬지의 힘
수리부엉이 날개 띄워 올리는 샛바람 일으키며
고사하고 난 뒤에도 줄곧 새순 피워 올리는 비수의 어린魚鱗

Wolsungwee's White Pine Recites Poems Wordlessly

Moving from Daekyuri of Seosan to Sinam of Yesan,
Where rich and broad plains spread,

Only for farming, building a house on halfway up the mountain Palbongsan,
    Kim Hongkyung was Chusa's great-great-grandfather, popularly
known as 'Handari Kim Moon'
    After moving here in neither mountains nor fields, he was appointed
to a prime minister,
    His son, Kim Hansin married king Youngjo's daughter, ennobled as
Wolsungwee, and given Wolsungwee Palace for the couple by the king,
    The house in white pine Village, now located in Tongeudong of Seoul

    The only place, where the white pines recite the poems on unyielding
noble beliefs
    The fresh white sprouts of the pine in Yesan, supposed to meet in the future
    Which will press to open the new era of liberal arts.
    Grow in the private field of Younggungri, Sinam

    The white pines of Younggungri coming from the ones of Wolsungwee
Palace
    Which symbolized Chusa's soul and body, and his life.

The treetop's power pushing at the peak,
    Makes the last wind pushing the wings of the eagle-owl, and
    Even after fading to death, sprouts the new leaves like fish scales stabbed.

영조대왕 어필비문御筆碑文

너른 평야 거느린 예산 구렁목 앞뜰
영조로부터 하사 받은 영지인 신암 터전에
왕의 딸, 화순옹주 시집오다
빼어난 기품의 월성위와 자주 영지에 들르다
열세 살 그 어린 나이에 시집온 옹주가
이십오 년 동안을 함께 살아온 남편,
서른여덟 살, 월성위 죽음에 스스로 곡기 끊다
왕은 상궁을 예산에 보내 곡기를 들라 명하였으나
동짓달 밤 동갑나기 옹주도 그예 절명하다
끝내 참척의 아픔 겪은 영조대왕이 붓 들어
붓을 들어 하염없이 울며
노쇠한 몸 겨우 가누며 비문 쓰다

* 화순옹주는 조선 제21대 임금 영조의 차녀로 사도세자와는 동복 누이동생지간이다.
  조선의 왕녀 중 유일하게 열녀로 지정되었다.

King Youngjo's Epitaph

Located in the front of Gooreungmok of Yesan with broad plains

The territory of Sinam given by King Youngjo

Became home to the beautiful princess, Hwasoon

Which she visited with her dignified husband, Wolsungwee.

The princess who married at 13 years old,

As soon as her husband sharing the married 25 years died

The princess aged 38 would give up food.

Though the king dispatched a court lady to Yesan and ordered the princess to take any food

At last, she died at December night.

The king, bereaved of his daughter picked up the brush

Crying incessantly, and

Wrote the epitaph with his weak body.

화순옹주 정려문

한 자루에 담긴 하나의 씨앗 움터
은장도 빼어 제 목 찌르다
지아비 죽자 곡기 끊고 뒤따르는 죽음에
고택 처마의 매서운 초봄 새싹이
살 떨면서 모시는 화순옹주 혼백
왕실호사를 마다한 결기 숨 쉬는
정려문 입구에 명줄 살아나
어명 거슬러 정념을 갈망한 순백의 순정이
지하 물살 밟으며 올라와
달빛에 다려 입은 생모시 바람치마

* 충청남도 예산군 신암면 용궁리에 남편 김한신과 합장되어 있으며 옹주의 열녀정문
  인 유형문화재 제45호 화순옹주홍문和順翁主紅門 또한 이곳에 있다.

Princess Hwasoon's Monument House

One seed in a sack sprouts and
Stabs its neck with an silver knife.
Over husband's loss, she refused all food and
Followed him to the grave.
The fresh sprouts under the eaves
Deified her spirit, shivering with the early spring cold.
Declining the luxurious royal life
Her purity was reborn into a monument house.
Contrary to king's command, her emotional pure love
Comes up, cleaving through the underworld river,
Worn the wind skirt of unbleached ramie in the moonlight.

채제공의 예언

입춘, 첫 새벽에 눈발 분분하더니 오전부터 오시는 비,
마늘 심은 채마밭에 한 아낙이 비 맞으며 일하고
가마를 멈추게 한 번암 채제공蔡濟恭 한양 추사 사가에 들다
입궐하는 길, 사모관대紗帽冠帶 비에 젖다
평소에 남인과 노론의 질시가 심하여 교우를 안 하던 터,
추사 부친 김노경이 크게 반색하며 정중히 영의정 대감을 맞는다
"아니, 각하, 연통도 안 놓으시고 어인 행차이신지요?"
"대문에 붙인 글씨는 누가 쓴 것이오?"
"저희 집 큰자식이 쓴 글입니다"
"이 아이는 명필로서 크게 이름을 떨칠 것이오
그러나 그리되면 운명이 기구할 것이니 붓을 잡지 못하게 하시오"
학식과 인품이 뛰어나 존경 받는 재상의 예언,
하나같이 고난을 담금질하여 빚어낸 혜안이나
장부丈夫, 세상에 한 번 태어나 어찌 일신의 안녕만 도모하랴
제주도와 함경도 고을 별강에 닿는 하늘채찍 갈기인가
고목 뿌리에 매달려 크는 유지매미 유충이 울자
채마밭 아낙의 치마 홍건이 젖어 그만 왼 몸매 드러나다

* 채제공(1720-1799) : 조선 후기의 문신. 벼슬이 영의정에 오른 명신으로 묘소는 청양에
  있다.

Chae Jegong's Prediction

Ipchun(first day of spring). On the day when the snow before dawn turned into rain in the morning,

When a woman worked in a garlic field in the rain,

Beonam Che Jegong, in a palanquin dropped into Chusa's house in Seoul

On his way to go to Court, gotten his dress suit rain soaked.

As two factions, Namin and Nohron were at feud,

Chusa's father rejoiced and welcomed him respectfully.

"Your Lordship, what brings you here without notice?"

"Who wrote the phrase on the door?"

"My older child did."

"He may be a master calligrapher,

If so, he will be doomed. So never let him pick up a brush."

The prediction by the prime minister, respected for his integrity and erudition

Shows his remarkable prescience achieved through various ordeals!

Yet, as a man, how does he only dream of success in his life?

Is it the whip's mane in the sky that can reach Hamgyong province and Jeju Island?

When the Larva of Large brown cicada growing from the roots of an old tree sings

The woman in the field happened to wear figure hugging skirt, all wet with rain.

여덟 살에 생부모를 떠나다

'여덟 살, 생부모 떠나
백부님 양자로 들어가는 길, 언제 다시 뵈올지요'

길가에 막 감꽃 피어나는 늦은 유월,
어머님은 끝내 소금 한 말 두 눈두덩에 넣으시고
보교步轎를 가로 막으려다
동구 밖 뒤편 감꽃 되시는 걸 보았어요

'여덟 살, 생부모 떠나
신암 농부들 밭갈이 황소 모는 소리 들으며
백부님 양자로 들어가는 길, 언제 다시 뵈올지요'

할아버지가 시동侍童을 붙여주셨고
지금 막 백부님은 개경유수로 행장 꾸리셔요
하지만 여덟 살, 생부모 떠나
아득한 거리를 연모라
무한히 애타는 사모라 소리쳐 부르나

'여덟 살, 생부모 떠나
백부님 양자로 들어가는 길, 언제 다시 뵈올지요'

* 백부 김노영이 후사가 없자 추사를 양자로 삼는다. 당시 김노영 벼슬은 개성유수다.

Leave Parents at Age 8

'At the age of 8, leaving my birth parents to be adopted by my uncle,
I wonder when I could meet you again.'

In late June, when persimmon trees bloom along the street,
My mother, shedding one mal of tears, and
Stopping the palankeen's way,
Finally became a persimmon flower, I saw.

'At the age of 8, leaving my birth parents,
Hearing Sinam farmers driving plowing bulls,
To be adopted by my uncle. I wonder when I could meet you again.'

Grandfather had me served by a chore boy, and
Uncle has just prepared himself for a journey to Gaegyeong.
At the age of 8, when I left my birth parents
A remote distance was affection,
The cry for poignant longing

'At the age of 8, leaving my birth parents to be adopted by my uncle,
I wonder when I could meet you again.'

비나리

- 추사 어머니, 기계유씨의 독백

사대부 가문의 일대장손인 너는 당당한 대장부,
네 두창 따위 조금도 두려워 말거라
네가 쌓아 갈 울창한 새벽 산맥 나는 알고 있노라

맨발에 봉두난발로 쓰러저 아산 헤맬지리도
내 생명집 옆구리에 탄생의 발길질해댄 너는
너는 내 양식, 빛나는 나의 깃발, 나의 긍지, 나의 명예

퉁퉁 불어나는 내 두 눈 영영 감을지라도
살쾡이 따위와 맞서 싸우지 말고 의연히 살아가는
너는 나의 영원한 꿈, 나의 장자, 나의 믿음
오석산 새파란 솔을 키우는 너는 내 뿌리

눈 크게 뜨라 싸워 가거라 몸 살펴 이겨 가거라
태풍 불고 칼바람 휘몰아쳐도 너는 나의 의지,
저승에서도 내 소망, 오직 너만이 내 생명이노라

* 두창 : 천연두. 추사는 유년시절 이 두창을 앓았다.

Prayer
- Mother's Soliloquy

You, the first son of the gentry family, are a noble man.
So, don't fear things like smallpox.
The dense mountains of dawn, you'll heap up, I'm seeing

Even if you wandered on bare foot around a hill with shaggy hair
You, kicking in my womb at birth
Are my good sense, my brilliant flag, my pride, and my honor.

Even though I closed my eyes forever,
You, acting honorably without fighting against the lynx-like people
Are my eternal dream, my first son, and my faith.

Keep up your spirits to fight and take care of yourself to win.
Though typhoons and biting winds blow, you are my will and
My wish even in my grave, and only you are my life.

평온, 반 평 #坪의 평온을 알라
- 추사 어머니 기계유씨의 당부

반 평, 나 태어난 자리는 반 평,
반 평, 나 후일 영면하여 누울 자리도 반 평,
넓은 집, 넓은 정원이 무어 대수냐
넓은 땅, 넓은 대지가 대체 뭐란 말이냐

'성천性天, 즉, 인성과 천도에 있어
가장 신비하고 심오하며 중요한 도리는
마음이 평온할 때만이 비로소 알 수 있음'이니
요란한 박수갈채에 마음 뺏기지 말라

세상 명리名利에 멀리 비껴 살며
'텅 비어 고요하고 욕심 없이 담박하여 적막에 거하라' 1)
무릇 이 말을 거울삼아 과욕을 버리라
마음과 몸을 평온에 두고 거하라

거듭, 반 평의 참뜻 깨달으라
평온, 반 평의 평온을 알라, 아들딸들아

* 성천 : 명나라 학자 여곤呂坤이 저술한 『신음어呻吟語』의 일부. 즉, '조화지정造化之精, 성천
　지묘性天之妙, 유정관자지지唯靜觀者知之, 유정양지계지唯靜養者契之'를 말한다.
1) 장자가 허정虛靜을 추앙하여 쓴 말.

Feel Peace in Half a Pyeong

- Mother's Advice

Half a pyeong, where I was born and raised
Half a pyeong, where I will lie forever after my death
What is a big house with a spacious garden?
What on earth is a large piece of land?

'性天', meaning that 'as for human nature and Providence,
You cannot realize the mysterious, profound order of nature'
Until you're in peace.
So don't be captivated by an ovation.

Be above riches and honor,
And be lonely with empty silence, living simply without avarice
Rid yourself of greed after the model of my advice,
And keep your soul and body in serenity.

Think over the true lesson of half a pyeong
Feel peace of half pyeong, my son and daughter!

* pyeong : counting unit area. about 3.3㎡

예산 화암사와 만나다

혹여 훗날 대처에 나가
먼지 자욱한 진창
그 막막하고 아득한 공허의 지경에 쓰러져
어디가 어딘지 사방 가늠 못할 때

숨결,
어릴 적 만나 고요히 사분거리는

부표浮漂,
임종 이후에도 눈에 확 띄는

칼바람 벼랑에 내몰려
모진 북풍한설에 정신 잃고 쓰러져서라도
아장아장 아기걸음으로 깨어나

새 아기 얼굴로 환하게
죽어도 다시, 다시 만나는 영혼나침반,
돌아와 끝내 재회할 원찰願刹

Encounter with Yesan Hwaamsa

Maybe someday in a strange city,
In the dusty mud,
When you feel so empty as not to know what to do, and
When you don't know where you are,

Breath,
Serene and affectionate, you met as a child

A buoy,
Conspicuous in death

On the edge of a windy precipice
Though you faint from the snow and cold wind,
You will recover and walk like a baby

With a creamy baby face
Born again after death and met again
The Temple, the compass for soul, destined to reunite.

* Hwaamsa : a temple in Yesan.

열두 살의 상주喪主

칠월에 월성위궁에서 양부의 혼이
시월에 종형 김관희의 혼이
섣달에는 할아버지가
서로 약속한 듯 우주의 별 되다

열한 살에 치룬 조모상까지
떠나가고 헤어지는 일에 찡한 코끝의 인연
새로 모시고 사는 양어머니와
생부모님과 두 아우 상희, 명희, 누이동생이 없다면야
한양 월성위궁이 다 무엇이랴
궁 담장 넘는 백송 살갗에
신암 고을의 낮달 스미어드는 아침결

열두 살에 이미 월성위궁 큰살림 도맡아
하인들 점고 뒤 삭망제 마치자
추사가 잡는 심중의 붓도 혼이다

A Mourner Aged 12

In July, adoptive father's soul
In October, his elder cousin, Kim Kwanhui's soul,
And in December, grandfather's soul, wearing lotus flowers
Became the stars twinkling up in the sky as if they promised.

At the age of 11, his grandmother's death
The fate ordained. Meeting and parting forever choked up.
Without the adoptive mother living together
His real parents and siblings, Sanghui and Myeonghui,
What would it have meant to live in Wolsungwee?
On the white skin of the pine over the fence
Shines day moon of morning.

Taking on Wolsungwee Place at age 12
Chusa, after identifying servants and finishing the regular memorial
ceremony,
Picks up a brush of soul.

정조, 붕어崩御하다

공동묘지 까마귀 떼 우짖는 소리인가
미국이 독립하고 영국의 아담 스미스가 '국부론'을 쓴
바로 그해, 병신년에 즉위하여
백성들에게 구체적인 혜택이 돌아가는 정치,
국가권력의 정당성을 획득한 왕이 붕어한 궁궐 뜨락,
작은 서까래 나부랭이들이 짓까불다
휘휘휘 바람소리 나다, 거센 폭풍우의 밤바람이여, 오라
와서, 조선 떠받치고 있는 백성 휘몰아가라
관리들에게 주리 틀리다 실신한
이 땅의 주인인 백성들은 언제 어느 시대나 짐승이라
허술한 요때기에서 뒹굴면 그나마 다행,
권력, 또는 원로라는 이름을 가진 괴이한 잡것들,
저 놈팡이들의 무지막지한 음심과 탐심의 노리개인 어린 백성을
도살하여 해저海底에 끌어넣어라
살아 있는 것보다 죽음이 평안한 시대다
부패의 균이 우글거리는 전쟁터 한가운데
늙은 홀어머니 혜경궁 홍씨를 두고
염천 시작되는 정해년 유월 스무여드레
폐허의 나뭇가지에 달린 위태한 왕국 지나쳐
개혁군주 조선의 왕, 정조 급서하다

* 정조 : 조선의 제22대 왕(재위 1776-1800). 추사 15세 때이다.

48

King Jeongjo's Demise

Is it cawing of a flock of crows?

When America achieved independence and 'The Wealth of Nations'
was written by Adam Smith

In the same year, 1776, king Jeongjo ascended the throne,

Governed his people well and

Consequently could legitimize his political power. On his passing away,

Such petty ones as rotten rafters acted up rudely in the palace.

Hui hui hui whistles the wind. Blow, a fierce night wind with rainstorm.

Blow to sweep the people supporting the country.

Tortured by government officials to swoon,

People, masters of the country were animals all the time

If only they had had a shabby mattress to loll around in, they would
have been fortunate,

The people who became a plaything

Of the vulgar fellows and greedy doyen with power

Kill and drag into the deep sea, winds.

It was when dying was happier than living.

Bidding farewell to his mother in a battlefield where corruption flourished

On June 28 of 1752 when the hot summer started

Looking at the palace hanging from the rotten bough

Joseon's reformation King, Jeongjo passed away suddenly.

* King Jeongjo : 1776-1800, 22th King of Joseon

붓꽃의 향연

- 추사, 첫 결혼

가슴 설레네 오월 붓꽃이 피고 오월 아침이 빛나네
수 차례 상주였던 열다섯 살 진중한 애늙은이 추사의 결혼대례일,
차령산맥 서북쪽에서 치달려온 가야산 산맥 한 줄기와
신암 팔봉산 소나무들이 월성위궁에 죄다 몰려와 상답보네
동갑나이 한산 이씨 문중 처녀의 신혼방에 그림자 시위 서네
충청도 고을서 한양도성 쩌렁 울린 이 추사 말고 또 있나
조선 소나무와 신암 소나무들이 서로 화답하며 침 발라 창호지 뚫자
추사, 그제야 머리맡 먹물 채 마르지 않은 화선지 밀치어놓네
단오절기 지난 경신년(1800) 오월 스무사흗날 밤이네
무작정 사모하게 하는 숲속의 꽃, 용산엔 나리꽃 천지인데
열다섯 살 헌헌장부 추사가 새벽 이슥해서야 새색시 금 족두리 벗기는
붓꽃, 한반도를 잉태한 추사 초례청은 온통 붓꽃 천지네

* 동갑나이로 추사와 결혼한 한양이씨는 1805년에 사망. 훗날 추사 묘소에 합장되다.

Iris Burst

- The First Marriage

The heart flutters. May. The iris blooms and the morning sun shines.

Chusa, at the age 15, who has played the role of chief mourner several times with great dignity, marries today.

One of the Gayasan that stretches out from Charyeong Mountain Range

And pine trees of Palbongsan come to help wedding.

His new bride, Hansan Lee of the same age sits in their couple room, and The door shadows of trees keep them safe.

Without Chusa, who else has stands astride Seoul?

When the pine trees from around the nation responding make a hole with spit on the Korean paper for a door,

Only then does Chusa put the wet Korean paper in the corner.

It is May 23 in 1800 after Dano, and

Trumpet lilies, the fatally attractive flower in a forest are overflowing in Yongsan

Chusa, the manly man of age 15, takes off the bridal tiara at the break of day.

Iris. His wedding hall is entirely filled with iris.

어머니 기계유씨의 유언

젖 먹던 네가 성근 이빨로 어미젖 물때
으스러지는 아픔에도 언제 네가 다시 내 젖가슴 물랴
영근 잇몸 대견해 살며시 힘주어 껴안았다
마지막으로 몇 마디 당부하는 이 말을 어미젖이라 알고
지금부터 내가 히는 말들 네 가슴에 새기라
잊지 말고 잘 새겨서 한평생 네 길이 되게 하라

정희야, 도처에 널린 게 독사굴이란다. 뱀 우글대는
정희야, 좋은 옷 입고 꿀보다 단 입술을 가진 여인,
세상 뭇 여인네를 조심, 또 조심하라 그곳은 독사굴이다
정희야, 또 금은보화를 내보이며 너를 호리는
맛있는 음식에 멋들어진 가무로 너를 흐려놓는
세상 뭇 유혹을 조심, 또 조심하라 그곳은 독사굴이다

장부로서 너는 금강석보다 강하고 굳센 의지를 가지라
장부로서 어둠을 후려쳐 혼돈의 세상을 밝게 하라
장부로서 너는 쉬이 네 입술로 고독하다 토하지 말라
장부로서 명리를 탐하지 말고 오직 의기를 키우라
장부로서 웅혼한 기운을 품어 웅비를 도모하라
장부로서 세상비판이나 평가를 떠나 오직 자존을 드높이라

설령 천애고아 같은 심중 고뇌의 파도가 밀려올지라도
죽든 살든 부모가 널 보고 있고 네 형제들이 있다
살아가기에 지치고 피멍든 옆집 이웃들의 유랑이 있다
손 발등 터지며 새벽부터 새벽까지 일하는 노비들 있다
새벽에 경건히 예불 올려 마음 씻어 학문을 닦되
외롭다, 쓸쓸하다, 괴롭다는 말은 입 밖에 꺼내질 말라
한 번 독사굴 빠지면 패가망신에다 목숨까지 잃기 십상,
바람이거나 아침 이슬, 혹은 연기에 지나지 않는 여인을
안개이거나 저녁 운무, 혹은 노을에 지나지 않는 재물을
검불이거나 새벽 박명, 혹은 티끌에 지나지 않는 명예를
안락, 그 하찮은 한 번 헛기침의 안일을 절대 탐하지 말라
쾌락, 그 하찮은 한 번 헛웃음의 미망을 절대 탐하지 말라
우주는 광활하고 역사는 광대하며 진리의 길은 광명하다
작고 사소한 일에서부터 진흥의 생명 씨앗 발아시켜
근면을 밑바탕으로 온화함을 근간으로 미소를 친구로
문중 식구들 잘 섬기고 존중하며 집안을 화목하게 가꾸라
시대를 앞서 읽는 혜안에다 변화와 개혁을 선도하라
그 어떤 일보다 가장 먼저 네 가족들로부터 존경을 받으라
한살이 생애를 살아내는 일은 누구나 지난至難한 일,
고난에 의연하고 환란에 굳건하며 평안에 잠잠하되
부디 내 몇 마디 말을 귀담아 듣고 부지런히 정진하라
명상과 고요에 잠겨 영원 해탈의 길을 궁구하라
나를 어미로 만들어 무한한 감격과 환희를 준
정희야, 내 가슴에 안겨 내 젖 물고 자란 내 큰아들아!

* 1801년 추사 16세 때, 36세의 기계유씨 사망하다.

Mother's Will

Whenever you, a suckling took the breast,
Despite the shattering pain as I knew that time would pass soon
I held you gently and strongly, taking your stronger gums admirable.
A few words I give you now
Keep in mind as if they were mother milk.
Dont' forget to make them a motto that lights your life.

Jeonghui, there is a snake tunnel everywhere, swarming with snakes.
Jeonghui, Beware of well dressed and honey-mouthed women, and
A sorts of women. Be careful as it may be a snake tunnel.
Jeonghui, be careful not to be enticed away by valuables,
By delicious dish, and stylish songs and dances.
Be cautious of a sorts of temptation as it is a snake tunnel.

As a man, make your will stronger than a diamond.
As a man, eliminate darkness and brighten the chaotic world.
As a man, don't express your loneliness.
As a man, have a splendid idea rather than riches and honor.
As a man, dream of great leap with sublime spirits
As a man, raise self-respect rather than be swayed by what others say.

When you feel a lonely orphan yourself filled with anguish

Your parents and siblings watch you whether they live or not,

Your neighbors being tired and bruised wander, and

Slaves work from morning till night with their hands and feet chapped and cracked.

Improve your heart and practice learning, having a Buddhist service devoutly at dawn, and

Don't say the words such as lonely, solitary, or painful

Once you fall into a snake tunnel, it is certain that you will ruin yourself or be killed.

Never be avaricious of the woman who is nothing more than a morning dew or smoke,

The fortune, nothing more than mist or sunset,

The fame, nothing more than morning twilight or dust, and

The comfort, nothing more than a trivial and complacent haw

Never be avaricious of the pleasure, nothing more than a illusion of a trivial pretend laughter.

The universe is vast, the history is extensive, and the truth is bright.

Let the seed of promotion germinate from small and trivial,

Let the smile be your friend based on diligence and gentleness, and

Serve your dear family and get along amicably.

With a keen insight, bring change and reform, and

Most of all, earn the esteem of your family.

To live a life is a very difficult thing to all men alike.

Face hardships with dignity and firmness, and be quiet in peace.

Please listen attentively to my some words and put them into practice.

Let the mediation and tranquility direct you to seek Nirvana.

Son, who gives me boundless joy and impression, Jeonghui

My son, who suckled in my bosom!

신유사옥辛酉史獄

조선국 하늘은 하나, 국왕이다 조선국 절대자는 한 사람, 국왕이다 허수아비라도 왕은 왕, 왕명이 국법이다 천주天主? 천주는 뭐 말라빠진 개뼈다귀냐? 혹세무민의 천주쟁이들 목 자르라 재판 거치지 말고 먼저 죽이라 덧붙여 이참에 눈엣가시 정적政敵들도 죽이라

회오리바람을 일으키시는 이여
피의 함성을 듣는 이여
일순간에 지나가는 생애를 살고 난 뒤
무고한 피비린내 뭉쳐야만
새 하늘과 새 땅이 열리는가요?

---

* 신유사옥 : 신유교난이라고도 한다. 1800년 순조 즉위 후 벽파가 정권을 잡자 천주교와 남인을 탄압했다. 1801년 천주교에 관여했던 남인 인사와 교회를 이끌고 있던 인물들이 대거 체포되어 많은 인사가 옥사하거나 처형당했다. 신자 약 100명이 처형되고 400여 명이 유배된 같은 해 12월에 척사윤음이 공표되면서 일단 마무리되었으나 이후에도 천주교 박해는 계속되었다.

Catholic Persecution of 1801

The heaven of Joseon is one. That is a king. The absolute in Joseon is one. That is a king. Though he is a puppet, a king is a king, and his command is a national law. Lord? Is Lord God a dried dog bone? Kill Catholics who delude the world and deceive the people. Without any trial, kill them unconditionally. Also, eliminate the political opponents, a thorn in our side.

One who creates wind funnels!
One who hears cries of the blood!
In life passing in a moment
Only a lot of blood of the innocent
Can open a new heaven and a new land?

* In 1801, Joseon Catholics were persecuted. Believers around 100 people were executed and exiled over 400 people.

장용영을 폐하다

바야흐로 지척 분간 안 되는 여름태풍 몰아쳤다
정조 사후에 열한 살의 어린 왕, 순조를 대신하여 증조할머니,
영조의 계비 정순왕후가 나라를 수렴청정垂簾聽政 하다
몸 가눌 수 없는 바람의 위력이 인마를 살상하는데
경주김씨 김한구의 따님인 대비는 사도세자를 폐한 벽파라
드러내놓고 정조 및 혜경궁 홍씨와 불화하다
새 정권 시작되자 정조의 동생 은언군과 시파를 죽이다
정조가 일평생 심혈 기울여 키워온 병영, 장용영을 즉시 혁파하나
지금의 수도방위사령부와 대통령경호실 직임의
조선 제일 최정예 강군이었던 장졸들이 일거에 흩어지다
바람은 이제 역사를 삼키다가 마침내 사랑까지 삼켰다
정조의 강군양성 계획도 단숨에 풍비박산나는 건 손쉬웠다
사실 이 때 이미 조선왕조의 운은 다하였으나
대왕대비는 드러내놓고 스스로를 일러 여군주라 칭하다

* 장용영 : 조선 후기 1793년(정조 17)에 왕권 강화를 위해 설치한 군영軍營. 정조가 승하하
  자 1802년(순조 2)에 혁파되고 말았다.
* 벽파와 시파 : 임오화변(1762) 장헌세자, 일명, 사도세자의 폐위와 사사사건으로 세자
  의 죽음이 당연하다는 벽파와 그의 죽음이 불행하다고 동정하는 시파로 분열되었다.

Abolish King's Army, Jangyongyeong

Summer typhoon, so strong that nothing could be distinguished even an inch ahead, raged.

After Jeongjo's death, for Soonjo, the little king of 11 years old, Queen Jeongsoon,

His great grandmother and Youngjo's wife in one, acted as regent.

Like a mighty wind, killing people at random

The queen, Kim Hangu's daughter who dethroned Prince Sado, Jeongjo's father,

Was conspicuously in conflict with supporters of Jeongjo and Crown Princess Hong, his mother

The new regime destroyed Jeongjo's brother, Eunen and the opposing faction, Sipa,

And reorganized Jangyongyeong, king's guard army that Jeongjo devoted himself to train, unhesitatingly.

As a result, belonging to capital defense command today

The officers and men of the most powerful army were scattered at one sweep

The insane gale swallowed its history and then love

The Jeongjo's plan to train the powerful army was smashed easily in a flash

At that time, when Chosen's luck had already run out

The queen great grandmother publicly claimed herself to be an empress.

단현斷絃

사 년여 전 한여름에 치룬 모친상에 자지러지던 일,
혼절한 옥체 끌어안고 밤 지새우던 그 밤에도
정신 깨어나 약한 몸으로 외려 내 눈물 훔쳐 주던 손길이
따스한 손길 고스란히 남아 내 얼굴 어루만지는데
에이, 고작 나이 스물에 엷은 미소조차 내 곁을 떠나
동갑내기 나만 남겨둔 채 습신 신고 용산 등성이 넘는단 말이요
섣달 눈발 휘날려 소나무가지 부딪치는 칼바람소리에
단현의 이 쓰라린 통증들 분분히 날리고
에이, 너무나 무정하오, 아주 말라버렸다오 내 눈물샘

* 을축년(1805년) 2월 12일, 한산이씨 사망(20세).

A String Snapped

When I fell into a swoon at mother's death 4 years ago

My love who held me stayed overnight, and

Dried my tears with weak but caring hands,

Whose warmness I could still feel on my face

At age only 20, alas, you and your smile left me

How could you leave me of the same age, wearing paper shoes over the ridge of Yongsan?

Snow flurried and biting winds of December shook the boughs of the pine tree

Thereupon, my poignant sorrow at the loss of wife flurried.

Gee, you're so pitiless! My lacrimal dried out.

* Chusa's first wife died on Febuary 12, 1805.

춤추는 신암 사람들
- 순조, 예산에 승지承旨를 보내다

홍천현감을 하던 추사의 생부 김노경이 문과에 급제하다
이미 흐드러질 대로 흐드러진 들국화 향기 짙은 시월,
며느리 잃은 슬픔 가시지 않은 시월이나
왕은 화순옹주의 손자인 김노경의 문과급제를 크게 반기다
왕이 직접 전례방前例房에 제수를 준비케 하명한 걸로 모자라
승지를 예산에 보내어 옹주 내외의 묘에 치제케 하다
이 날 예산 향저는 한양에서 내려온 승지와 하객들로 북새통 이루다
이월 추위에 부인과 사별한 추사의 고요는 뒷선,
가을 추수를 모두 마친 예산 들녘에 사람들 붐비고 붐벼
처음으로 왕실 음식을 맛보는 신암 뜰 흥겨워 춤추고
예산고을 초목도 이날 온종일 어깨동무하며 풍물 쳐댔다

* 승지 : 조선시대 승정원의 정3품 당상관. 왕명을 출납하였다.
* 전례방 : 조선시대, 호조에 딸려 있던 부속 기구. 종묘, 사직의 제사 때 드는 제물과
  왕에게 바치는 진상물, 사신의 행차 때 보내는 방물 따위에 관한 일을 맡아보았다.

Sinam Folks Dancing
- King Soonjo Sends a Government Officer to Yesan

As a Hyeongam, having moved to Hongcheon in Gangwondo
Chusa's birth father passed the state exam.
In October, when the fragrance of camomile flowers in profusion
was strong, and
He couldn't still get out of the grief for his daught-in-law' death.
But the king rejoiced to hear of the news that Hwasoon's grandson passed.
Therefore, he ordered the authorities concerned to prepare food for a rite,
Sent a government official to Yesan to perform religious rituals.
On that day, hometown in Yesan was bustled with masses the official
and guests.
Neglecting quietude for Chusa bereaved in chilly February
The fields in Yesan after harvest were jammed with people.
Sinam folks danced merrily and tasted the royal food for the first time
All trees and plants of Yesan also played pungmul(instrument)
enthusiastically, putting arms around.

* Hyeongam : a person of junior 6th rank who governs small settlements or communities

건재고택

집 짓는 일, 간단하지 않다
겨울 눈보라, 여름 폭풍우에
온기 불어넣어
생명요람 짓는 뼈의 역할

사소한 일 아니다
사람이 사람을 생각하는 일

잠 못 들고 염려하며
연모하다 스스로 명주실 뽑아
고치 속으로 들어가는 일

* 건재고택 : 충남 아산의 설화산 아래 자리한 외암리마을의 중심부에 '영암집'이라고
도 부르는 고택이다. 조선 후기 사대부가의 전형적인 건축으로, 건물의 배치와 규모·
기법으로 보아 외암리 민속마을을 대표할 만한 주택으로 추사의 처가집이다.

Gunjae Old House

To build a house, it is not simple
Into both winter snowstorms and summer heavy rain
Inspiring warmness
To make the foundation for the cradle of life

It is not trifles
That is to think another human being

Wakeful nights worrying
Pining away and with silk from his body
To make a cocoon to come into!

* Yean Lee lived 'Gunjae Old House' before marriage.

추사의 홍조紅潮

비밀 문인가, 저승 물줄기 넘쳐나 연속되는 헤어짐
월성위궁에 같이 살던 양어머니 남양홍씨
양어머니마저 운명하여 장례모신 뒤끝
김노경이 통정대부에 이르자 추사 혼처 서두르다
일문의 혼사란 어른들 뜻이 중한지라 무진년 가을
양모 복중服中임에도 추사 재혼이 이뤄지다
추사보다 두 살 아래인 스물한 살의 온양 처녀, 예안이씨
해맑은 얼굴에다 고운 마음씨로 평생 추사를 섬긴 여인
달 없는 밤에는 달로, 해 없는 낮에는 해로
추사를 섬기며 추사를 비춰온 추사의 분신으로
평생 오로지 추사 단 한 사람만을 위해 살다가
훗날 추사보다 일찍 운명하여 한 없이 추사를 울린 여인
추사, 살아 있건만 유배 중이라 생이별한 여인
이 여인을 아내로 맞아들이는 젊지만 중후한 신랑,
평생 이 여인을 가슴에 품은 긴 부리의 해오라기 신랑,
신랑인 추사 입가에 빛나는 정채精彩 보아라
차령산맥 아침 햇살이 빚어내는 붉디붉은 추사의 홍조

* 예안이씨 : 무진년(1808) 충남 온양 송악면 외암리에서 당대 명문 집안인 이병현을 아
  버지로 태어나 21세 때, 추사와 결혼하여 34년간을 추사와 살았다.

Chusa's Face Flushed

Was it a secret door? Family members continued to die as if Lethe overflowed.

When even Namyang Hong, the adoptive mother, living together in Wolsungwee

Passed away and held a funeral,

Kim Nogyeong hastened to look for a spouse for Chusa.

In Autumn of 1808, yielding to family seniors' decision,

Chusa re-married in spite of the mourning period

His spouse, Yean Lee was from Onyang, younger than him by 2 years

With a bright face and a tender heart, she was devoted to Chusa all her life.

As a moon on moonless nights and as a sun on cloudy days

Woman, taking care of him like his avatar and

Living only for him in her life.

Woman, who made Chusa cry as she predeceased

Woman, separated from him by exile

The groom, young and dignified, who marries the woman

The groom, who hugged her to his bosom forever.

Look at his lively smile,

Chusa's flushed face glowing in the morning sunlight.

제2장

조선의 금강경

추사의 사행단 행보에서 대과급제까지

The Most Excellent Sutra of Joseon

From Diplomatic Mission to the Pass of the State Examination

조선의 금강경

날이 막 밝아온다 미지의 먼 나라 휘돌아
어두컴컴한 새벽 말없이 걸어온 숲 속 나무들
무덤 깨워 목숨 일으키며 오다
죽은 목숨은 없다 잠자는 몸도 없다 백년이 백 번 지나도
한 번 산목숨은 다 아침햇살이다
밤새워 상수리나무 진액 핥는 장수풍뎅이 날개 쳐대고
눈부신 나신 훤히 드러낸 채 배불러오는
나무 그루터기는 일제히 배동바지,
붓대 생명 폭풍우에 껴안은 몽당붓으로
시, 서, 화, 경학, 고증학, 금석문, 불교학의 심경心經심지 태워
가뭇없이 내거는 생명 등불이
화암사 아름드리 기둥 돌며 타는 무현금

Joseon's Most Excellent Sutra

Day is just breaking from the undiscovered country.

The bushes are walking silently out of darkness

Reviving a person in the grave.

Nobody is dead. Nobody is sleeping. Though tens of thousands of years have passed,

All of beings that were once animate are morning suns.

A beetle's flapping its wings, licking the sap of oak, and

The tree stump naked is exposing a growing baby bump,

It's when the rice plant, start bearing grains simultaneously!

Holding a stubby writing brush in storm

Burning the wick of poetry, calligraphy, paintings, chinese classics, historical research, monumental inscription, and buddhist studies

The lamp of life lit unperceived in darkness

Plays the Geomungo without strings, circling a large wooden column of Hwaamsa.

관심觀心
- 추사 아버지의 말

충신이 간언을 안 하면 나라가 위태롭고 간언을 하면 자신의 몸이 위태롭게 된다 이를 간파한 이는 당태종의 명신, '위징魏徵'이다 연약한 체구지만 굳센 의지와 바른 말로 위징은 늘 이 세 가지 거울을 들어 왕을 간했고 당태종이 혼란한 정국을 안정시킨 연유는 귀에 거슬리지만 충언을 수용한 때문이다

너는 경전을 마음 중심에 심되 네 마음을 보라
스스로 존재를 살펴 네 스스로 마음을 보라
관심, 마음거울 가꿔가는 이 관심을 잘 새기라

* 관심 : 수신修身에 관한 유가의 아홉 가지 덕목 중 하나로 정좌관심靜坐觀心에서 따온 말. 어떤 욕망 어떤 생각이 자신의 마음과 영혼을 지배하는지를 살펴보는 일.

* 위징(580-643) : 중국 당의 정치가로 유명한 「술회述懷」라는 시를 읊음.

* 당태종의 거울론 : 以銅爲鏡, 可以正衣冠, 以古爲鏡, 可知興替, 以人爲鏡, 可以明得失. 즉, '청동을 거울 삼으면 의관을 바르게 할 수 있고, 옛것을 거울 삼으면 흥망성쇠를 알 수 있으며, 사람을 거울 삼으면 이해득실을 밝힐 수 있다.'

Introspection
- Father's Advice

If the faithful subjects don't expostulate, the nation will be in crisis, and if they expostulate, their lives will be in danger. This was a saying of Weisheng, a well known statesman in Tang. Though he was weak, with a strong will and truth, Weisheng expostulated to his king giving three examples. The king could stabilize the chaotic state of affairs because he accepted Weisheng's expostulation harsh to the ear.

Examine your own thoughts keeping the aphorism in mind.
Analyse your own ideas, studying yourself.
Introspection! Bear in mind to keep the mirror of your soul clean.

사행단使行團

'길에는 주인이 없다. 오직 그 위를 가는 사람이 주인일 뿐이다.'[1] 실로 길을 걸어가는 일이 생애라 길을 떠나지 않고 어떻게 일문을 일으킨단 말인가 길을 떠나지 않고 어떻게 장도長途의 웅대한 대지를 알 것인가 먼 길을 떠나지 않고을 어떻게 피 끓는 청춘을 다스려 넓은 세상의 진기를 알 수 있단 말인가 가족과을 고향이라는 안락한 길을 떠나지 않고 어떻게 거대한 세계의 찬란한 문명을 호흡한단 말인가 길을 달려보지 않고 어떻게 신선한 흙바람을 마신단 말인가 동짓달에 한양을 떠나 명년 봄에야 귀경하는 사행단에 몸담지 않고 어떻게 천고의 소리를 일깨워주는 위대한 영웅들의 공간에 들어설 수 있단 말인가 길을 달리지 않고 어떻게 웅혼한 천지신명의 울림을 들을 수 있단 말인가 청운의 웅지와 기개 넘치는 추사의 연경 사행단 합류는 청년추사에게 있어 일생일대 최대의 모험이자 흥분이며 찬연한 합주의 서곡이자 기묘하고 신비스러운 내세의을 내세에 대한 개문開門이라,

    달려, 연경에 닿기까지 삼천리 길 달려
    흥분한 압록강 물살 데리고 광활한 요동벌 지나
    쉬지 않고 두 달 동안을
    연경 밤하늘 수놓은 수묵水墨의 질타,
    '조선 국력 약해지고 백성들이 궁핍해진 원인은 학문에 있다'[2]
    체험과 견문 통한 학문적 가설을 설정,
    조선을 부강한 나라로 만드는 전망 보려
    달려, 추사라는 자수정에 닿기까지 달려

1) 조선후기 실학자, 여암 신경준(1712-1781)의 말.
2) 연암 박지원의『북학의 서』에서 인용.

74

A Diplomatic Mission

'Nobody can possess a path. Only the person who walks on it is its owner.' To live is to tread the path! How can he bring honor to his family without leaving home? How can he see the grand world without going a long way? How can he realize the real value of the broad world controlling young blood without setting off on a long journey? How can he experience a worldwide splendid civilization without leaving his loving family? Without running the path, how can he breathe in dust? How can we go into the place of the greatest heros that have ever lived without attending the diplomatic mission that will be back by next spring, leaving from Seoul in November? How can we hear the voice of the gods without running the path? It was an adventure of a lifetime, excitement, prelude of ensemble and opening the gate to the next life that Chusa attended the diplomatic mission to Beijing.

Run! Dash in a breath three thousand ri till Beijing.
Cross the excited Amnokgang and pass Liaotung
Keeping running for 2 months.
Outcry of Korean ink spreading over the night sky of Beijing.
'The weakened national power and people's difficulties stemed from Learning'.
To set up a academic hypothesis based on the experience, and
To see prospect of a prosperous country
Chusa keeps running till the amethyst.

추사, 압록강을 건너다

고향 땅 예산을 흘러온 푸른 숨결들인가
압록강에서 퍼지는 천고의 역사가 저마다 숨 쉬다
백두산 뚫고 생겨나와
압록강이라는 이름과 언어를 가진 문화로 흘러
'아전들은 어지러이 강가에서 전송하며
내년 봄 잘 돌아오라 다투어 인사하는' [1]
도강渡江하며 과거의 해석이 미래를 지배하는 힘이라는
음성 새겨들으며 예산 고을도 압록강을 건너다

1) 홍양호의 1782년, 「강을 건너며渡江」에서 인용.

Chusa, Cross the Amnokgang

Are they the azure breaths flowing out from his hometown Yesan?
Each of millennial histories breathes dispersing on the Amnokgang
Running through Baekdusan
They become a culture called Amnokgang.
'Petty officials at the river see off in a muddle,
Scrambling to say 'bon voyage'.
The words, 'to controls the future, it's important to analyze the past'
Marking, he along with Yesan crosses the river,

청나라 구련성九連城에서의 일박一泊

- 사방에서 들려오는 물결소리에 뒤척이며 듣는
  서릿바람 불어대는 구련성 이곳에는
  한밤중 물결소리 나그네 꿈 뒤흔드네
  애간장 끊어지는 강가 언덕 아니어도
  나그네 이 소리에 저설로 다징해리[1]

남북으로 길게 산맥 산봉우리 열어
겨우 벽돌 몇 장 정도의 성城흔적 간직한 구련성九連城,
연달아 서 있는 아홉 개의 성이 있던 이 고을에서 사행단이 묵다
벌써 겨울 추위가 몰려오는 동짓달 초순
추사, 구련성에서 생애 첫 이국의 밤을 새다

---

1) 조선시대 시인이자 문예비평가인 남용익의 저서『호곡집』권12,『새상곡십사절塞上曲
   十四艶』중「구련성」에서 인용.

Stay Overnight at Camp Guryeonseong of Qing China

- At Guryeonseong where a chilly wind blows, and
  The sound of water is heard all around,
  The dash of the waves at midnight wakes the dream of a traveler
  tossing and turning.
  Like the riverside where the heartwrenching parting happens
  At the sound of it, his heart becomes tender spontaneously.

On the mountain peaks running from north to south
Stands Guryeonseong which shows the trace of a castle only with
several bricks
  The diplomatic mission stays in town having 9 castles, standing in a row.
  In early November when cold winter has already set in
  Chusa stays overnight abroad for the first time in his life

견마잡이

달려갈 것이다 내 고삐 내가 잡고
예산 땅 정기 세워
몽당붓이라도 조선 제일가는 붓촉 돼라
조선학예 견마잡이로
정신 불 밝히는 조선의 새 빛 돼라

A Horse Handler

I will run holding the horse by the reins.

To make Yesan spirit stand.

I will be the nation's best calligrapher.

As the handler of Joseon arts

To brighten nation's soul I will be a new light.

동복童僕을 껴안다

- 사람과 말들을 성처럼 둘러놓고
  해 저물자 소리치며 서로를 부른다네
  물가에는 임시로 주방 설치하고
  때때로 산을 향해 뿔피리 불어댄다
  앉으면 윙윙대는 모기떼가 괴로워도
  누우면 쏟아질 듯 은하수가 기뻐하네
  이역에 와 있음을 밤들어 실감하니
  함께하는 동복과 더더욱 다정해라[1]

사행 길에 뒤따라와 시중드는 동복을 보며
등촉 밝혀 서로 어깨를 껴안은 추사,
옛 선비가 구련성 노숙 읊은 시편을 읽다

* 동복 : 사내아이 종.

1) 조문명(1680-1732)이 1725년에 쓴 「유전에서 노숙하며」를 인용.

Hug a Boy Servant

- People and horses stood in a circle like a castle.
  They yelled each other as night fell,
  Temporarily arranged kitchen at waterside, and
  Facing mount, blew a horn at times.
  Mosquitoes buzzing were annoying, yet
  The galaxy brimful of stars overhead was sheer joy.
  After dark, on Chusa's fully realizing that he was in a foreign land
  The boy servant traveling with him looked even more valuable.

Staring at the boy attending to him throughout the trip,
Chusa lit a lantern and held his shoulder.
The old scholar read a poem about sleeping outside at Guryeonseong.

산해관에서

장부는 여기서 비로소
제 몸 살펴보며 몸을 쉬고

웅장, 장엄한 것은
천길 벼랑 아니다
벼락 치는 천둥소리 아니다
예산, 예산의 꿈이
꿈틀대며 똬리 튼
연모의 마음 밭이다

* 산해관 : 1381년 명의 명장 서달이 관문을 개축하고 산과 바다 사이에 위치한다 하여 산해관이라 칭했다. 오늘날에도 만리장성에서 가장 잘 보전된 관문들 중 하나로 남아 있다.

At Fortress Shanhai-guan

A man finally relaxes
And rests in here.

Magnificence. Sublimity is
Not a bottomless bluff and
Not the roll of thunder, but
The heart of love,
Where Yesan's dream
Coil, wriggling

---

* Shanhai-guan : Shanhai Pass, a mountain pass of the Great Wall of China Shanhai-
   kuan District, in Qinhuangdao, Hebei, China.

완원阮元과 사제의師弟義

어둠이 빚어내는 별빛 물고 핀 매화,
향기 소슬한 이국의 밤바람은 매서워도 그윽하여
아무도 본 사람 없지만 참 좋아한다
낯선 늑골에서 돋아나는 학예의 새파란 이끼여
가히 해동제일통유海東第一通儒가 분명하나
시대를 뛰어넘어 파종한 이 말은
좋아한다는 말, 포옹한다는 얼거리 마디는 매혹이라
홀로 자생하는 첫 순정의 매혹,
완당阮堂이라는 당호를 받은 황홀한 꿈이다
심각하다 삶이라는 이랑은
아름답거나 피투성이거나 죽었거나 살았거나 간에
신선하고 신비한 아침 전율이라
추사, 청나라 석학인 완원의 제자 되다

* 완원(1764-1849) : 추사의 스승이자 중국 청대의 학자. 완원이 주창하였던 '실사구시'는
추사의 사상 정립에 절대적인 영향을 끼쳤다. 추사는 완원으로부터 '해동제일통유'라
는 미칭을 얻었고 또한 추사가 자작하였다는 이설도 있으나 완당이라는 당호를 받
았다.

Establish Master - Disciple Ties with Ruan Yuan

Korean apricots, blooming with stars shining in the darkness,

With its fragrance is filled the lonely foreign country night despite biting winds.

Nobody has seen it but everyone likes it

Deep blue moss of arts, springing from the strange ribs,

Indeed, it must be "海東第一通儒", meaning he was the best confucianist of Joseon.

Which transcends the ages.

Roughly speaking, to love, or to hug is fascination and

Captivation of the first love, growing naturally,

To get a nickname, Wandang, it is a charming dream.

Serious is furrows of life

Whether it's beautiful, bloody, alive or dead

It is a fresh and mysterious morning thrill.

Chusa, be a disciple of Ruan Yuan of Qing

* Ruan Yuan : Scholar of the Qing China. He had an influence on Chusa' thoughts.

실학의 춤

　고종황제가 당한 한일강제병합이 아니더라도 임진왜란, 조선이 완패하여 한양도성은 왜군들 차지, 놀란 선조는 도망치다 관노들과 백성들이 던지는 돌멩이 맞다. 어가御駕는 풍랑 일렁이는 바다의 조각배, 분조分朝라는, 조정이 둘이라는, 왕이 둘이라 백성이 도탄에 빠졌는데 다시 두 차례의 호란胡亂이 겹쳤다.

　실학을 주창하면서 먼저 반계 유형원이 춤추자
　가슴 뜨거운 홍대용, 박지원, 박제가를 거쳐
　정사가 아닌 자제 군관들이나 연행사燕行使 수행원들이
　연경 오가다 개혁과 변화를 꿈꾸며 일어나 춤추는

The Dance of Korean Practical Learning

Prior to Japanese annexation of Korea under the reign of Emperor Gojong, Japan invaded Korea in 1592 and successfully took Seoul. Meanwhile, reighted Seonjo ran away flustering and was hit with stones by people. His carriage was a boat on the stormy sea, where the royal court was divided into two, having two kings. The people fell into a state of distress and, what is worse, two Manchu invasion occurred.

Bangye Yu Hyeongwon started to dance, advocating Silhak,
Followed by Hong Daeyong, Park Jiwon, and Pak Jega with enthusiastic zest
From military family and entourage to visit Beijing. Not political affairs
But traveling made them open their eyes to reforms and changes.
Then they had a dream and stood to dance.

옹방강翁方綱과 맺은 사제의師弟義

왜 그런지 친밀하다 낯익다
몸에 느티나무 키우는
일흔 하고 여덟 살의 스승이 들려주는
'나는 옛 경전을 즐기느니라' [1]
보소재寶蘇齋에서 들리는 천둥소리를
한 청년이 무릎 꿇어 받는다
'경술문장해동제일經術文章海東第一' [2]
느티나무 스승이 주는 글귀를
스물다섯 살 추사, 옷섶 여며 받자
말씀의 수면에 튀는 잉어,
살아 펄떡거리는 기이한 필담이
미친 듯 조선을 휘감아 치다

* 옹방강 : 청나라 법 첩학의 4대가로 꼽히는 금석학金石學, 비판碑版, 법첩학法帖學에 통달
  한 학자 겸 서예가.
1) 옹강강이 추사에게 한 말.
2) 1810년 정월 29일, 옹방강이 추사를 처음 만나 필담을 하면서 한 말.

Establish Master - Disciple Ties with Weng Fanggang

I don't know why I feel intimate and familiar.

Taking after a zelkove

The master of 78 years old tells

'I enjoy classic books'

The thunder sound from Bosojae

A young man receives kneeling.

Zelkove master's phrase, '經術文章海東第一'

Chusa of 25 takes, adjusting his dress.

A carp jumping over the water of the words.

An eccentric conversation by writing, flopping alive

Resonates all over the nation frantically.

* Weng Fanggang : Scholar of Qing China. He had an influence on Chusa's Arts.

이 무렵의 조선 노비奴婢

호ㅑ를 이룰 수 없다, 그냥 구ㅁ다
사람이 아닌 그저 입 하나일 뿐이다
그런데도 온갖 공역과 온갖 궂은일은 도맡아 하다
주인의 호적에 올려져
물건으로 통용되어 주인집에 사는 솔거노비牽居奴婢,
외부에 살지만 언제든 달려와 신역을 제공하는 외거노비外居奴婢,
관청에 두고 부리는 관노官奴 등등으로
인격권이 부여되지 않는 노예다
물건으로 취급당하며 살기 고달파도
그렇다고 분노를 모르는 건 아니다
임진왜란 땐 관노들이 선조의 어가御駕를 향하여 돌 던지다
뜨거운 피돌기의 애정 또한 깊어
몸 부서져라 시달리고도
움집에 들어선 흐벅지게 껴안고 격렬히 입 맞추다
뜨겁다, 최소한 거짓 없이 정 나누는
조선의 최 하층민 조선노비는
(사랑을 속이고 옆자릴 속이는 자는 들으라)
가족 간 애틋하게 사는 조선의 풀뿌리,
신역 고되지만 진한 조선의 힘이다

Joseon Slaves Back Then

Slaves could not have a family register. They were only a chattel.

They were not humans but just goods.

Nevertheless, they undertook all the public service and dirty work.

Added to their master's family register

The household slaves living in their master's house as chattels,

The free servants who lived outside the master's but did labor anytime, and

The slaves working in a government office and so on

All were ones without human rights.

Though objectified and all worn out

They were not unaware of feeling resentment.

During Japanese invasion, they threw stones at the royal carriage

Also, from hot and deep affection

Even after exhausted by labor

On returning to their hut, they held and kissed passionately.

Hot. They shared real feeling.

The lowest class in Joseon

(The man who deceives his lover and betrays his neighbor, hark)

Was grass roots of the nation with family love

Joseon's real power while their lives are hard.

보담재寶覃齋

한양에 돌아오자마자 추사가 자신의 보담재를 둘러보다 이미 사행단
의 일원으로 연경에 가기 이전에 추사는 월성위궁 서재 가득히 오랫동
안 사모해 온 옹방강의 책과 탁본들로 도배를 놓다시피 옹방강을 흠모
하여 보담재라고 당호도 미리 지어두었던 서재명이다 옹방강과 절친한
친구의 호를 본따 미리 추사라는 자신의 호도 정해 두었다 옹방강을 만
난 추사가 그런 필담을 드리자 옹방강은 파안대소하였다 추사가 그 주
인공인 옹방강을 실제로 만나고 돌아온 그 떨림의 마파람이다 한양 월
성위궁 감싸는 청나라의 신화, 담계覃溪의 경학이 놀아대는 마파람에 황
매화 일제히 앞다퉈 꽃망울 터트려 꽃잎 각자刻字 향기 짙다

* 보담재 : 추사가 스승으로 모신 청나라의 담계覃溪옹방강翁方綱이 소동파蘇東坡를 보배롭
  게 모신다는 뜻에서 지은 당호인 보소재寶蘇齋를 본받아 옹방강을 보배롭게 마음에 담
  는다는 뜻에서 '보담재'를 자신의 아호로 삼고, 다시 이를 서재명으로 삼았다.

Bodamjae

On returning home, Chusa looks around his Bodamjae. Long before he went to Beijing as a staff member of the diplomatic mission, Chusa who admired Weng Fanggang decorated his study room in Wolsungwee Palace with his books and rubbings and called his room Bodamjae after Weng Fanggang's pen name. Also, he adopted the pen name Chusa after Weng Fanggang's great friend. Afterwards Weng Fanggang who talked about the story wiht Chusa by writing laughed out loud. Chusa must have been really excited because he met the figure he admired in person. The south wind blowing from excitement along with the myth of Qing and Chinese classics surrounded Wolsungwee Palace and then the yellow apricots burst into bloom, scrambling. Strong is the scent of the letters engraved on the petals.

* Bodamjae : Chusa's library. Meaning is 'Weng Fanggang is precious'.

봄 아지랑이의 싹, 유당酉堂

스승 옹방강이 써준 현판, 유당
물 대는, 생명수 흐르는 집이라
추사의 시, 서, 화의 뿌리인 가친의 당호,
봄 아지랑이 골짜기 가로질러와
고택 동산에 봄 싹 틔우는 금잔디

* 유당 : 추사 가친의 아호이다. 추사는 청나라 서울 연경(현재의 북경)에서 스승 옹방강에
  게 부탁하여 선친의 아호 편액을 선물 받는다.

Buds in Spring Haze, Youdang

Youdang, a signboard that master Weng Fanggang wrote for him
Means a house irrigating life-saving water.
And it's also a pen name of his father's, from whom Choosa's poery,
painting
and calligraphy started.
Spring haze comes across the valley, and
Gold grass on the hill sprouts.

흙, 꿈을 꾸다
- 옹방강의 석묵서루石墨書樓

청나라 제일의 눈알맹이들
청년 추사의 넋을 뺏는
수만 권 장서와 기이한 자료로 뒤덮인
고령의 스승 옹방강 서재,
돌아보건대 조심할 일이다
생전에 무얼 자꾸 건립하지 말 일이다
청나라 보고인 석묵서루,
추사 학예의 도화선이 된 이 석묵서루가
손자에 의하여 훼파되었으니
땀 흘려 애쓴 것이
결국 소멸하여 한 줌 흙,
흥분과 애착도 한낱 흙 아닌가

* 석묵서루: 옹방강의 서재. 추사는 부친이 1809년 동지사절단으로 사행 길에 올랐을 때, 군관자제의 신분으로 연경을 방문해 청대의 석학 옹방강을 만난다. 당시 추사의 나이는 24세이요, 옹방강은 78세의 노인이었다. 젊고, 기백이 넘치는 추사를 만난 옹방강은 자신의 서재 석묵서루石墨書樓에 보관된 서화와 장서, 탁본들 8만점을 보여주었고, 이 때 옹방강은 추사를 일러 '학문과 문장이 해동의 제일이다經術文章海東第一'라고 극찬하였다.

Dirt, Dream
- Weng Fanggang's Library

Old master Weng Fanggang's library,

Which bewitched young Chusa

Filled with tens of thousands of books and bizarre materials

The best of the best things in Qing China.

In retrospect, it should have been avoided

To build something in his life

His library, the treasure house of Qing,

Which gave the impetus to Chusa's art and science,

Which his grandson dilapidated.

Though made with efforts

It went back to a handful of dirt.

So did excitement and attachment.

목리木理의 길

생부께 절 올리고 고향 신암 가는 길
흙먼지 길 말갈기에 걸린 하늘 어깨에 메고
월성위月城尉 양위 묘에 절 올린다
선조 음덕으로 생원시 일등 합격하여 왔나이다
내 입술 받아주는 상석 앞에서
엎드려 술잔 붓고 절 올린 스물네 살의 추사 울다
가을걷이 끝난 십일월 들판 까치들이
예산 고을 추사 눈물 찍어
바다 멀리 제주도와 함경도 북청 향하여 날고
장부 일생에 어찌 고난이 없으랴
새 학예의 길에 어찌 안녕만 구하랴
원圓둘레 나이테 무늬 내며 길을 묻다

* 추사, 생원시 장원급제하다. 1809년 11월 9일. 순조 9년,
* 목리 : 세로로 자른 나무의 표면에 나이테로 말미암아 나타나는 무늬.

Tree Ring's Direction

He bade farewell to his father and left for hometown Sinam,

Carrying the sky hooked by horse's mane on my shoulder, raising a cloud of dust

After making a deep bow before his ancestors' tombs

Chusa of 24 years old wept while pouring a drink

In front of the ceremonial stone table

Thinking that he passed first in the examination thanks to the ancestors' hidden virtue.

In November, Magpies in the field where the harvest was completed

Dipped into his tears and then

Flied away to Jeju Island and Buckeong in Hamkyungdo.

How could a man wish not to experience sufferings in his life?

How could we wish not to be in predicaments in pioneering a new art and science?

The direction is asked on the tree ring.

귀하디귀한 평생지기, 초의

- 초의선사와 만나다

선을 창시한 달마조사와 견줄 초의선사 서 계시네

초의艸衣, 무위자연의 풀옷이란 법호를 가진 사내

고승대덕인 온호玩虎스님을 계사戒師로

구족계와 법호를 받은 초의대선사는

불경과 선禪, 노자, 장자, 범서는 물론 시, 서, 화에 통달하다

서른 살 동갑의 나이로 추사와 교유를 시작한 이래

염불, 범패, 탱화, 단청, 바라춤에 능통하며

추사와 평생지기로 살았던 한국 차[茶]의 중시조

한 사람이 어찌 그리도 다재다능하며

한 사람이 어찌 그리도 박학다식하단 말인가

추사의 유배 시절 가장 큰 힘이 되어 주었다가

추사가 운명하자 예산에 달려와 호곡하며 제문 올린

달마조사가 중국에 있다면 조선엔 초의선사 계시네

* 초의선사(1786-1866) : 호는 의순意恂, 초의艸衣이며 추사의 평생지기로 시, 서, 화, 다茶에
  정통하여 사절로 부리는 당대의 명사로 추사가 30살 때 동갑나기 초의를 만났다.

Valuable Lifelong Friend, Choui

- Meet Choui Seonsa

Choui Seonsa stands, compared to BodhiDharma, the founder of Zen.

The man with a Buddhist name, Choui meaning 'clothes nature made'.

From a high priest, Onho, received the commandments of Buddhism,

Then bhikku, and Buddhist name. Choui Seonsa

Mastered all kinds of Buddihist scriptures, Zen, Taoism, mediocre

books, poetry, paintings and calligraphy.

He was the same age as Chusa, and they met first at aged 30.

Choui, the reviver of Korean tea and a life long friend of Chusa were

Proficient in Buddhist prayer, Buddhist chants, altar portarait of

Buddaha, Dancheong, and bara dance.

How could one man be versatile?

How could one man be well informed?

He who gave great encouragement to Chusa in exile,

Ran to Yesan, wept aloud and delivered a funeral oration at his death

The Korean person Like Bodhi Dharma in China was Choui Seonsa..

낙엽의 얼굴을 보며
- 경상도 감영에서 월성위궁 아내에게 띄운 편지

언제나 종종걸음을 본다오
나를 위하여 새벽부터 새벽까지 애쓰는
하나하나 표정들이 눈에 삼삼하오
경상도 관찰사행 부친 따라
사나흘 지났을 뿐인데 집 생각이라오
나는 아무 염려 마오
외처의 풋정이야 닳고 낡아빠진 안질_{眼疾}
어찌 규방 댓돌과 비하리오
오로지 가친 곁에 서는 것만으로
든든하고 기쁘기가 헤아릴 수 없구려
뒹구는 낙엽의 얼굴 가까이
당신 계신 한양을 바라본다오

Looking at the Fallen Leaves

- A Letter Written to Wife in Wolsungwee from Gamyeong, Gyeongsangdo

I always see you scurrying and

Serving me from dawn till night.

Your memories vividly recur to me.

After I left home with my father, a governor bound for Gyeongsangdo

In only three or four days, I miss you

Don't mind me.

Light affection toward a strange woman is like a chronic eye disease

How dare can it be compared to the doorstones of the main room?

Just being with my father

I feel happy and confident.

The fallen leaves rolling

Remind me of you.

소봉래小蓬萊의 아침

비원을 품고 있는 비산비야 오석산이
금강산의 별칭, 봉래산蓬萊山
스승 옹방강의 당호 소재蘇齋를 합하여
스승을 공경하여 지은 보소재라
옹방강의 소蘇를 차용하여 소봉래라 이름 할까
용궁리 추사고택 등성이 너머
오석산 병풍바위 휘돌아 소봉래 살고
화암사 요사체를 일러 소봉래각이라며
추사, 진달래주 마시는 술잔에
새벽 바다 붉은 빛이 어둠을 깨며 온다

Morning in Sobongnae

Oseoksan, neither mountain nor field, embracing a secret garden.

Combining Bongnaesan, byname of Geumgangsan

With Sojae, pseudonym of his master Weng Fanggang,

Bosojae was named to show respect to his master.

Similarly, is it called Sobongnae by borrowing 'So' from Weng Fanggang's pseudonym?

Over the hill behind Chusa's old house in Yonggungri

Sobongnae lives around Oseoksan screen rock.

Calling Hwaamsa Sobongnaegak,

Chusa drinks azalea wine, and into the glass

The rosy glow of the dawn sea comes, breaking darkness.

추사와 정약용丁若鏞

섬광의 번쩍임인가 진심은 기막히게 진심을 안다
진정으로 사모하는 이들은 상대의 마음을 안다
우주가 숨겨놓은 이 비밀한 영감靈感은 거듭
상대방이 자신을 포옹하는 줄 먼저 온몸으로 알고
자신을 기망하는 일도 꿰뚫어 안다
생각은 사람의 일이 아닌 인격의 일이고 영혼의 일이라
무려 스물네 살이나 연상인 다산이 추사에게 쓴 편지,
추사가 다산에게 쓴 편지글이나
다산의 몸이 병들어 신음하다 운명하는 절명의 순간에도
서로가 서로를 알아 모시는 진심이
진심으로 서로에게 다가섬을 읽는 이 풍경,
섬광의 황홀경인가 고요하나 즐거이 심금 울리다

* 정약용(1762-1836) : 조선 후기의 실학자, 유형원·이익의 학문과 사상을 계승하여 조선
  후기 실학을 집대성했다.

Chusa and Jeong Yakyong

Is it a flash of light? The truth can astoundingly recognize the truth,
The lovers who truly love each other read each other's mind
The secret inspiration the universe hid
Feels with its body that the other embraces it over and over and
Sees through his deception also.
Thoughts belongs not to man's affairs but to his personality and soul.
The letters that Dasan 24 years older than Chusa
Exchanges with him, show
Even until Dasan fell ill and died
They sincerely recognized each other.
Heartily to cotton up to each other
Is it an ecstatic flash? It pulled at heart silently but cheerfully

추사, 아들 얻다

청초하고 기이한 칠월 꽃,
시와 그림에 능한데다가
미소로 휘장 드리우고
단지 눈길만으로 붉은 심장 불 지르는
맵시 고운 소실, 권씨
걸어 다니는 난꽃 자태에
오석산 홍겹다
사랑하는 이 여인으로부터
추사, 아들 상우를 안는다

Chusa, Have a Son

How elegant and eccentric the flower of July is.

With great talent in poetry and painting,

Smiling faintly,

She would set on fire to heart, just if beholding.

Concubine, Kwan looking smart

Oseoksan is pleased

With the walking orchid

Chusa's lovely women

Bore a son, Sangwoo.

아침의 꿈
- 아들, 상우를 품에 안고

무릎에서 내려놓지 않는 핏덩어리,
옹알이하는 어린것아
아들아, 나를 비로소 아비로
나를 아비로 만든 건 강보에 쌓인 너,
가슴에서 내려놓지 못할
아들아, 너는 나의 불전佛典,
칠월 아침 나팔꽃,
환하게 빛나는 너는 나의 꿈이라

A Morning Dream

- Holding Son in His Bosom

A newborn baby on my lap
Cooing and gurgling.
Son, in swaddling clothes
Who made me father.
Not putting down in my bosom easily
Son, you're my Buddhist scriptures,
And the morning glory of July morning
Shining brightly, you are my dream.

추사, 간난이 말을 듣다

- '동짓달 칼바람이 휘몰아치곤 했다
  더러는 식구들 잠든 머리맡으로 얼어붙었다 녹은 물이
  뱀처럼 스멀스멀 소리 없이 기어들어오곤 했다
  옷을 껴입었다
  한 평이 채 안 되는 방 안이라도
  두터운 솜이불만으로는 냉기를 견딜 수 없다
  그 기억의 창가에 어리는 아스라한 날들의 반짝거림 스쳐
  숫돌에 벼려지는 조선낫의 날빛,
  더러 이리떼가 나타나 송아지를 물어가도
  찬 방바닥에 놓인 한 줌 주먹밥이
  혹한보다 독한 세상 추위와 맞설 수 있는 힘을 주었다'

어두컴컴하거나 숫제 안 보이는 언어,
어린 딸 둘을 돌보아주는 여종인
안채에 딸린 방에서 추사, 간난이 말을 듣다

* 추사는 소실로부터 아들 상우 외에 딸 둘을 슬하에 두었다.

Chusa, Overhear Gannani's Talk

- 'November biting wind would blow.
  The frozen water in a bowl by his pillow would melt and
  Ooze through it silently like a snake.
  In a room less than a pyeong
  Putting on layers and
  Covering myself with a thick cotton-stuffed blanket weren't enough to
  bear a cold.
  A sickle glitters, sharpened on a whet stone
  The glimmering light on the window reminded me of dim memories
  Sometimes a pack of wolves caught a calf, and
  The rice ball on the cold floor
  Gave energies that could endure the colder life'

Dimmish or pitch dark talk.
The woman servant, looking after his little two girls
Gannani's talk Chusa in his room overhears

* Gannani is a babysitter.

추사의 대과급제

나라의 우두머리 관리가 되려면 반드시 거쳐야 하는 문,
정계 뛰어들어 한바탕 걸쭉하게 놀아볼 양이면 서야 하는 판,
옹방강을 만난 이후 옹방강에 심취하여 공부만 하다가 옹방강 사후
기묘년 서른네 살에 이르러 추사, 대과에 급제,
어사화 꽂고 증조부 월성위 묘에 올리는 절,
국왕이 직접 월성위 봉사손에게 궁중의 제례물품을 하사하는 풍경을
먼먼 시간을 걸어 올라와 숨어 있는 운명이
신암 고택 석정을 때려 일순 다시 샘물 멈추길 반복하던 사월,
향후 이십여 년 지나 이 대과급제로 목숨이 위태로울 줄 뉘 알았으랴
사월이면 사월마다 봄을 집어삼키는 황사바람 드세다

* 옹방강 1818년 사망.

* 기묘년 : 1819년

116

Chusa Passes a State Examination

The gate which one must pass to be a top manager, and

The stage which one must come on to engage in politics hard.

Chusa who was absorbed in study, fascinated by Weng Fanggang

Passed the state examination at age 34 only after his death.

A deep bow made to his great grandfather's grave, wearing the
paper flowers that the king gave on his hat

With court ancestral rituals items given by the king.

Meanwhile, the fate walking from a faraway past was hidden.

In that April, the spring water spouted and stopped repeatedly

Who knew that the pass in the state examination might put his life
at risk in around 20 years?

Every April, the strong sand wind sweeps spring

제3장

조선의 해걷이바람

추사의 대과급제 이후부터 의금부 하옥까지

Dark Clouds

Frim Political Career to Imprisonment

조선의 해건이바람

막이 열리자 쉴 새 없이 막이 흔들리고 있다 사람의 만남과 헤어짐,
뼈아픈 하루를 아우르며 노루목 빈 가지에 석양이 걸려 있다
햇살 따스한 수양버들 아래 노는 봄 물고기 떼 사라지고
어느덧 하늬바람 가고 된바람 품에서 뜨는 개밥바리기 별빛이여
이미 오래선 준비되어 자리한 해질녘 하늘 운부여
옆, 옆자리, 옆 사람, 가장 가까이 코 맞대고 사는 사람의
막이 내리다 막이 내리고 있다 사람과 사람의 만남과 이별이 흐른다
제주 해변의 드센 바람 굽이치는 파도 이랑에 이별의 눈시울 붉어
한 발 한 발 내디딘 발자국마다 고인 통곡의 막 내리다
인연, 거품 인연이건만 꼭 껴안고 더 울지 못하였구나
같은 하늘 아래에서 같이 살아온 날들의 미욱한 흐느낌 자국들,
영욕이야 실상 뜬세상 잠시잠깐 스쳐 부는 마파람,
옆, 옆자리, 옆 사람이 나의 조상, 나의 분신, 나의 신神이자
나의 미래, 나의 나, 단 하나 나의 연모, 나의 영생 아닐까
시작하라 다시, 다시, 다시, 시작하라 다시 개혁하고 변화하라
정결히 옆 사람을 신으로 섬기는 일, 다시 그 한 가지부터 시작하라
다시 새로워져 마음 영토에 새 나라를 세우라, 다시 개국하라
해 지고 낮 동안의 분주한 일들이 북청고을 겨울 열매로
죽음을 목도하면서 살아 눈 멀거니 뜨고 막막한 유배길 가는
막이 열리다 생이 흔들리는 사이 조선 별빛 사위며 부는 해건이바람

Dark Clouds

The curtain opens, but it sways constantly meeting and parting.

The evening sun sits on a branch above the footpath, finishing a painful day.

A shoal of fish swimming in the warm sunlight under a weeping willow are gone.

Evening stars, shining in the strong wind after a west wind

Fog at sunset, prearranged a long time ago

The person who lives face to face beside me, close at hand, close to.

The curtain drops. The curtain is dropping. The meeting and parting between the people meanders.

Shedding parting tears on the Jeju beach with violent winds and whipped waves,

A wailing curtain drops at every step one takes.

Relation. Even if it was a bubble relationship, they should have held tightly and cried more.

The days they've lived together under one sun, the traces of stupid tears.

Glory and shame is like a south wind sliding by in the transient life.

Is the person beside me, close at hand, close to, my ancestor, other self, god,

My future, myself in me, only one affection, and eternal life?

Start again, once more, again. Start over again. Reform and change!

Start from serving the person beside me as a god, with a pure heart.

Found a new nation in your mind, and open a country again.

The sun sets and the busy day changes into winter fruit in Bukcheong.

Watching the death with big round eyes, on the way to gloomy exile

The curtain opens. While the life shakes, a dark wind blows, removing Joseon's starlight

꿈을 필사하다
- 추사의 동몽선습童蒙先習 필사본

'천지만물 가운데 사람이 가장 귀하다'[1]
동몽선습의 첫 장 첫 구절은 그렇게 시작된다
태어난 지 채 사 년도 안 된 아이, 상우야
신새벽에 일어나 내가 직접 붓 들어 베껴 썼다

아비의 탄생 약 일백여 년 전 거슬러 올라가
영조가 서문 쓰고 송시열이 서평 쓴
중종 조에 박세무가 쓴 이 동몽선습을
아이야, 아랫목에 잠든 나의 아기야
아비는 네가 열심히 읽고 그 가르침에 따르길 빈다

너는 모든 사람 가운데 내게 가장 귀하다

가마솥 밥알 익히는 저 장엄한 우주의 중력을 알라
너를 껴안고 밤새워 내 꿈을 필사하다

* 동몽선습 : 조선 중종 때 학자 박세무가 저술하여 1670년(현종 11)에 간행하였다. 《천자
문》을 익히고 난 후의 학동들이 배우는 초급교재.
1) '天地之間 萬物之中惟人最貴 所貴乎人者以其有五倫也(하늘과 땅 사이에 있는 모든
것 중에서 오직 사람이 가장 귀한데, 사람이 귀한 까닭은 오륜이 있기 때문이다.)'에
서 인용.

Copy a Dream

- Chusa Copies Dongmongseonseup

'Man is the noblest of all creatures in the world',

Says the first verse in the opening chapter of Dongmongseonseup

My little child, aged less than 4 years old, Sangwoo.

I copied this book for you at dawn.

100 years before I was born

Pak Semoo wrote this book in King Joongjong's reign

With the preface written by King Youngjo and the prologue by Song Siyeal.

Son, sleeping on the warm spot.

I make a wish that you will read hard and keep in mind.

Your are the noblest of all men in the world.

You should know the grand gravity of the universe that cooks rice

Holding you in my bosom, I transcribe my dream.

* Dongmongseonseup : Introductory Textbook.

달의 궤적

- 너는 열심히 읽고 가르침에 따르며 정밀하게 생각하고 힘껏 실천하라.
  그래야 사람의 도리에 이를 것이니 부디 열심히 공부하라. 초승달 뜨고
  사흘이 지난 밤, 아비가 쓰다. [1]

꼭 기익해라 상우야
저 초승달이 곧 보름달이다
공부하는 일은
초승달이 보름달이 되는 첩경이자
살아 누리는 최고의 복,
사람의 사랑을 아는 유일한 가치이니
늘 글을 가까이 하라
아비가 없어도 옆에 있는 듯이
힘껏 궁구하라
아가, 힘찬 내 아들아

1) 추사가 필사한 〈동문선습〉에 추사가 직접 쓴 발문.

Moon Phases

- After reading hard, you should think deeply and put in action depending on its teachings. Only then will you do your duty. Make sure to study hard. On the 4th day after a new moon arose, your daddy writes.

Sangwoo, don't forget
A new moon will be a full moon.
Learning is
A shortcut to a full moon,
The best luck, and
Only value through which you can know the love for human.
Always read a book.
Whether I were not around you or not
Study hard.
Sweetie, my energetic son.

맹독을 깨끗이 하라
- 추사의 충청우도 암행어사 출사

탐관오리貪官汚吏란 거머리들 득실거리는 세상이다
주민 고혈 빨아먹는 습성이 인이 박인 이 말거머리들이
인허가의 도장을 움켜쥐고는
의무 없는 의무의 멍에를 씌워
밤낮없이 주릴 틀어대는 개망나니의 땅이다
고대광실에서 개기름 번지르르 흘리며 저들이 살고
예나 지금이나 수탈이 이어지다
그를 모르는 자들은 아직 강보에 쌓인 어린아이와 멍멍이뿐,
만면에 웃음 띠며 헛기침소리 크지만, 보라
저들 창고엔 곡식이 넘치다
은밀히 숨겨놓은 첩실 분단장하기 바쁘다
저들이 잉태하는 건 독 품은 독사들,
이 땅의 독사들이 뿜어내는 맹독을 깨끗이 하라
낳고 자란 충청우도 암행어사로
왕이 쥐어 준 마패를 가슴에 품고 맹렬히 말 달린다

Remove Deadly Poison

- Chusa Proceeds to Chungcheongwoodo as a Secret Royal Inspector

Corrupt officials like a leech are rampant across the nation
Who squeeze out the blood of the people habitually.
As exclusive licensors
They impose unnecessary duty on people and
Bully them all day and night like a world for louts.
Their face being greasy, they live in a palatial mansion.
Exploitation is the same now as in old times.
All the people know them except a baby in swaddling clothes and a dog
Look at the corrupt officials with a broad smile, hemming.
With grain is filled their warehouse, and
A secret concubine is busy powdering.
In their belly grow venomous snakes.
Remove the poison snakes release.
To Chungchengwoodo where he was born and grew
Chusa pelts, holding a special pass given by the king.

악연의 실타래

일거에 오십 초반의 김우명,
비인현감을 봉고파직함은
태안군으로 암행 출발하기 전에
사십대 초반의 추사가
충청우도 암행어사로 나가 어사직분을 수행한 일,
그러나 뉘 알았으랴
훗날 그가 사간원의 대사간이 되고
동문 파당인 김홍근이 사헌부 대사헌으로
실권 장악하여 백관을 감찰하다가 실타래 옭죄어
끝내 가시울타리 두른
한 번 악연은 끝까지 맹독이라

* 대사간 : 조선시대 왕에 대한 간쟁을 맡은 사간원의 장관으로 정3품 당상관직.
* 대사헌 : 조선시대 사헌부의 장, 종2품이다.

Skein in Ill Fated Relationship

Chusa in his early 40s

Dismissed a local magistrate,

Kim Woomyung in his early 50s,

Before he left for Taeangun,

Which Chusa did as a secret royal inspector in Chungcheongwoodo.

However, who would know

That the magistrate would be appointed chief censor to speak frankly to the king in person, and

That Kim Honggen, his alumnus in a faction, would be a director to investigate and punish the officials' illegalities but finally be in prison

Caught in a snare?

Once an ill-fated relationship, always deadly poison.

한겨울의 축수祝壽
- 부친 김노경의 회갑연

정성 다해 꿇은 두 무릎
낳아주시고 길러주신 은혜에 감읍하며
하늘 받들듯 섬겨 모시니
부디 천수하소서 평안하소서
호조참판, 경상감사, 형조판서, 이조판서, 예조판서, 공조판서,
대사헌, 병조판서, 한성판윤이란 관직 거쳐
판의금부사로 계신 가친을 뵈며
동짓달 눈 쌓인 월성위궁에서 아버님,
조정대신들과 여럿이 모여
설레는 마음으로 충청우도 암행어사인 소자,
마흔한 살의 정희 절 올리니
부디 천세 천세 천천세 누리옵소서

130

Long Life Wishes
- At Father's 60th Birthday Party

Sincerely falling on my knees

I shed tears of gratitude for bearing and rearing me.

Intending to serve you like a god

May you live a long and blessed life.

My father who served in various high-ranking government posts and

Is currently the head of Royal Investigation Bureau

Your son aged 41, the secret royal inspector of Chugncheongdo

Makes a deep bow excitedly

With the ministers

At Wolsungwee Palace covered with snow in December

May you live a long long life!

* Uigeumbu : Special judicial bodies

추사의 금관조복

- 원손 탄생 진하시陳賀時 선교관宣敎官 되다

원손 탄생은 조선왕조의 경사慶事
나라의 큰 경사 시에 왕의 조서를 읽는 선교관
정3품에 가자加資되어
통정대부에다 당상관이 된
마흔두 살의 추사
칠월 햇살이 추사의 금관조복을 들추다

Chusa's Royal Court Uniform

- He Reads the Congratulatory Message of the Birth of a New Crown Prince

It's a happy occasion in the royal family that the crown prince's son
was born.

Promoted to the third-grade official,

That reads a royal message,

Doubling as Tongjungdaebu and Dangsanggwan

Chusa of 42 years old

July sun raises his court attire.

가문의 전성기

추사가 아버지 김노경의 회갑잔칠 열던 그해 겨울
흰 눈발이 자주 오석산에 휘날렸다
사랑방 손님들이 들끓던 그 해,
암행어사인 추사와 판의금부사인 가친의 권세는
당당하고 늠름하여 광영이 극에 날했다
사람들은 이때를 전성기다 추사 가문의 권력과 영광의 시대다
추사 가문의 정점이라 말하지만, 아니다
얼마 안 있어 추사가 제수 받은 벼슬, 예조참의와 동부승지도 아니다
가친의 고금도 위리안치 시부터
추사 가문의 전성기는 그 고난의 때부터 시작한다
환란 시 불붙는 정신불의 흰 촉수가 전성기다

Glory Days of His Family

In that winter, when the birthday party for Chusa's father was held,

The snow often flurried in the Oseoksan, and

The reception room was crowded with guests.

Chusa and his father hired for the key positions

Looked brave and imposing, and his family was at the summit of

its prosperity.

People say that time was the era of power and fame and

Glory days of his family, but it's wrong.

The summit of its fame was not also the higher positions given later.

It started when his father was exiled to Gogeumdo.

The glory days were when the spirit rising above adversity blazed.

추사의 평양행

예조참의에서 물러나 있을 때다
가친이 평양감사를 제수 받아 봉직하던 평양엘 가다
이미 금석학과 학예의 대가이자
미래를 보장 받는 시선이 추사에게 몰리다
거칠 것 없는 사내부의 호기에나
금강산 절경만큼이나 매혹적인 여인들 늘비하다
대동강변 부벽루에서 추사, 대취하다

Travel to Pyongyang

At the time he resigned from a royal secretary

Chusa went to Pyongyang, where his father worked as a governor

of Pyongyang.

Known as the master of epigraphy and calligraphy and

A promising politician, Chusa arrested the people' attention.

In there were man's gallant spirit, nothing to fear and

Attractive women compared to the grandeur of Geumgangsan.

He was dead drunk at the Bubyeongnu on Daedonggang.

선계의 여인

- 추사, 평양 기생 죽향을 연모하다

치명적인 눈빛 보라
매혹, 노래와 춤사위에
시와 그림 치는 아이 처음이라
뭇 남자와의 가창은 멋,
너를 만난 이후로
아무 것도 안 보이고 오로지 나는
너에게 빠지다
너 없이도 너를 만나는
너는 비밀의 여인,
나를 만나러 지상에 내려온
선계의 여인, 죽향이여

Heaven Woman
- Chusa Loves Jukhyang, Gisaeng of Pyongyang

Look at the fatal eyes.

Fascination. I've never seen the woman like you, having abilities

To compose poetry and paint as well as sing and dance,

To sing together with a strange man is like a morning dew.

Since I met you

I have been blinded and I was

Only enchanted with you

Seeing you without you.

You're a secret woman,

Who came to see me.

Jukhyang, sent from heaven

Gisaeng : Korean geisha

노루목 목단
- 추사, 동부승지 되다

단청丹靑 짙다

목단牧丹 붉다

열강列强의 함성소리 조선을 흔들다

삼정三政에 빠져

유리걸식하는

어린 백성 떨건 말건

궁궐 단청 붉다

아무런 일 없다

묵은 텃밭에

목단 홀로 지다

* 동부승지 : 조선시대 승정원의 정3품 당상관. 왕명의 출납을 담당하였다.
* 삼정三政 : 전정田政 - 조세제도, 군정軍政 - 병역제도, 환곡還穀 - 구호제도.

Peony in Norumok

- Chusa, Be a Official in Royal Secretariat

Dancheong is deep colored,

Peonies are red, and

Shouts of the powers shake the nation.

Because of real estate taxes, military service, and grain policy

Wandering out aimlessly,

Poor people

Are trembling, yet

The dancheong of the palace is still red, and

Nothing happens at all.

In an old vegetable garden

Peonies fall off alone.

* Dancheong : traditional multicolored paintwork on wooden buildings.

허련을 제자로

초의대사 손을 잡고 방문을 두드리다가
헛기침해대며 그림 치는 환쟁이야
수정 냇물이 네 가슴에 흐르고 있음이 훤하니
부디 정진하여 일가를 이루라
내 아들처럼 여기는 소치, 내 제자야

* 남종화가의 대가 소치 허련은 초의의 소개로 추사의 문하에서 그림 공부를 할 수 있
  었다.

Place Heoryeon as a Disciple

When I knock a door, holding Choui Seonsa's hand

I can see the brook in your heart

As a painter, hemming

Devote yourself to establish your fame.

Sochi, my disciple like my son.

* Sochi : Heoryeon's pen name

가화家禍의 서곡

작은 불알 달고 나온 놈이
혹은 큰 불알일 수도 있지만 놈이
남 물어뜯고 할퀴며
있는 말 없는 말 중상모략 한창이다
밤낮 호색질 모자라
선비들 후려쳐 벗겨 먹다
재물 뺏기 이골 난
한양 동네 주름잡는 머리털 허연 망나니에다
그 음흉한 몸뚱이 내둘러 춤추는
음탕 방탕 허탕 잡탕놈아
나는 늘 즐겁다 야아
내 안에 등 푸르른 들판,
내 안에 숨 쉬는 시냇물,
갓난아이 미소 있다
모를 거라, 화는 나의 복이다

* 추사에게 봉고파직 당한 구원具涙이 있는 부사과 김우명이 지돈령부사로 재직 중인
추사의 아버지 김노경을 탄핵하는 연명상소를 거푸 올리자 왕은 처음엔 김우명을 유
배 보냈으나, 빗발치는 대소 신료들의 상소에 지쳐 경인년(1830) 10월 2일, 마침내 순
조는 당시 65세인 김노경의 고금도 유배를 명하여 김노경은 여기서 4년여 유배생활
을 한다.

A Prelude to Family Disasters

With two little balls

Or with big balls

A guy bites and scratches

Indulging in slandering.

He copped day and night.

In addition, he wheedled scholars out of money.

Used to tricking others out of money

The frenzied lout with white hair

Dances shaking his treacherous body.

You, lewd, lustful, lecherous, and littery.

Yay, I am always happy.

A green field and

A brook murmuring

Baby smiles are in me.

You never understand, anger is good luck to me.

부친 김노경 유배당하다

- 추사의 고금도행

황망하여 상투 풀어 젖힌 채 달려왔습니다

통곡하다 쓰러진 아내를 안방에 눕히고

말갈기 치며 수백 리 달려, 물길 수백 리 달려왔습니다

해풍, 벌써 한기寒氣 가득한데

가마우지 섧게 날아다니는 섬마을 외진 움막이 따스합니다

화조도 병풍 대신 걸린 삼베 메나리에

썩은 등잔대 훈훈하고 불살 향기롭습니다

밤바다 은물살 내는 밤이 평안하고 고요합니다

한양보다 더 빛나는 별들 가득합니다

마주 앉아 먹은 저녁밥,

밤하늘 저리 청신하고 가슴 이리 맑습니다

황망히 다시 온 길 되짚어

물길 백 리 산길 백 리 수백 리 길 되돌아왔어도

섬 세모래 밭 감싸는 그윽한 아버님 눈빛의 곡기穀氣

찰지고 여물어 월성위궁도 든든합니다

* 고금도 : 전라남도 완도군 고금면의 섬, 가친의 위리안치 이후 추사는 모든 관직에서
  물러나 조용히 학예의 연찬을 하다가 고금도에 내려와 부친을 모셨다.

146

Father in Exile

- Chusa Leaves for Gogeumdo

I came running in a flurry, with my topknot untied.

My wife cried herself to collapse in the room, and

I came running hundreds of ri, whipping a horse

Sea breeze. Cold feeling was full, yet

Warm was a remote mud hut of an island where a cormorant flied

crying out.

On the wall were hanging Hemp and water parsley in stead of a

flowers and birds painted folding screen.

The decayed lamp prop was warm and the light smelled sweet.

The night sea shimmering in silver was calm and peaceful.

The sky were studded with the stars shining more brightly than in Seoul.

After having supper sitting face to face with you

I felt refreshed in the clean sky.

Although, in a hurry, I retraced my steps

Traveling 100 ri of mountain path and 100 ri of waterway

Your lively eyes staring at seashore fine sand

Encouraged me in Wolsungwee reassured.

부친의 너털웃음
- 고금도 귀양지에서 김노경이 한 말

신암 사가私家의 우물 두레박이다
섬에 작은 두레박 샘 있어
고금도에서 그런대로 가시울타리에 기대다
별 기력도 남아 있지 않다만
굳이 벼슬이니 이름을 내세울 것 있느냐
이미 잘려 나간 혀와 이름,
여기저기 짓밟히고 짓무른 상처 안고 살 거다
뿌리 뽑으려 한다면 뿌린 뽑힌 채로
이대로 저대로 되는대로
버티고 버텨 말똥구리처럼 뒹굴 거다
나뒹굴어져 자빠지는 거, 고거 제일 멋진 거라
염려 마라 질긴 고래심줄 목숨이다
불태워 씨 말리려 해도 좋아
신암 두레박 샘물 맛
아랫배 뱃심 단단해지는 물맛 참 좋다

Father Smiles Loudly
- His Exile to Gogeumdo

It looks like the well bucket of hometown house.

On this island is a little well, and

That provides a thorn fence for me to lean against.

I, sackless, don't want to boast my fame and position.

My tongue and name have already cut, and

I will get on with the wound trampled underfoot and festered.

If I were rooted out, with my root out

One way or another, at random

I will roll over to survive like a tumblebug.

Falling down to roll around is the most fantastic thing.

Dont' worry. My life is as tough as a whale sinew.

Though the entire family are wiped out, I don't care.

The water of the bucket well in Sinam

Tastes good so as to get the nerve.

옹인달 편지

옹방강이 죽고 그의 아들이 죽고
옹가 잇는 옹인달은 추사를 의부로 존칭하다
청나라에는 옹방강이 있고
옹수곤이 있어 금석학의 뼈대를 이루는데
요질한 옹수곤과 동갑인 추사 일어서서
문풍지 소리인가, 누군가 부르는 소리
부르는 소리, 낯익은 소리 들으며
후다닥 툇마루 나서니 폭설이다 눈 오는
새벽 눈 소리에 실려 오는 얼굴만 살아나다

The Letter from Weng Yinda

After Weng Fanggang died, his sons all also died.

His grandson, Weng Yinda called Chusa a worn father

Thanks to Weng Fanggang and

His son, Weng Shukun, the foundation of epigraphy could set up in Qing.

The sound of paper weather strips or someone calls?

The sound. Hearing something familiar

Chusa stands up, and

Runs to the floor to find it snowing heavily.

At dawn, the sound of snowing brought the face of loved one to his mind.

격쟁擊錚

임진년 이월에 한 번, 구월에 한 번
궁궐 앞 꽹과리의 외침을 들어라
아버지의 고금도 위리안치는 너무나 억울하다
내가 마흔일곱 해 동안 살면서
가친께서 과히게 처리하신 일 본 적 없다
이 징소리는 나의 목숨 건 상소다 죽어도 좋다
추사의 격한 외침이 왕궁에 퍼져
부친은 이듬해 해배되어 돌아오다

* 임진년(1832) 2월 26일과, 9월 10일 두 차례 추사는 임금 행차길에 꽹과리로 임금께 직
  접 호소하는 방식으로 송원하였다.

Gyeokjaeng

Once in February and once in September of 1982

Hear a shout from the gate tower of the royal palace.

It is wrong to banish my father to Gogeumdo.

While I've lived for 47 years

I've never seen he misused his power.

I risk my life to beat the drum

Chusa's outcry reverberates around the palace, and

His father returns home in the following year

* Gyeokjaeng : When the king goes out, someone who has chagrin beats a gong to
  appeal.

홍경래의 난亂

무과시험에 낙방하였지만 나, 홍경래의 나이 마흔,
마흔, 사내대장부로서 일국을 취할 수 있지 않겠는가
곪아터진 조선 왕조를 뒤엎을 수 있으리라
무학둔재無學鈍才라도 권문세가의 자식들만 급제하는 나라,
삼정의 문란에다 관리들 수탈이 드센 나라,
나라가 위급존망에 처하면 함경, 평안도의 사람을 쓰고는
주요 관직엔 기용치 않는 불평등의 나라,
마흔, 불과 다섯 달 만에 붉은 몸뚱이 쓰러졌어도 홍겨워라
평서대원수, 나, 홍경래의 세상은 오고 시대는 개벽하리라
누군가 반드시 내 뒤를 이어 봉기할 것이라
나는 죽지만 죽어도 죽지 않을 것이라
마흔, 오늘에 이르러 뭐를 더 바랄 것이냐 대원수여!

* 홍경래(1771-1812) : 평남 용강 출생. 홍경래는 세도정권의 부패정치, 삼정의 문란 등 사
회적 모순에 저항하여 1811년(순조11) 조선왕조의 전복을 목표로 한 농민반란을 일으
켰다. 각지를 유랑하는 동안 지배층의 부패상과 백성들의 비참한 생활을 체험하면
서 사회의 모순을 인식하게 되었다. 1800년(순조 즉위) 우군칙과 함께 가산의 다복동을
근거지로 삼아 군사훈련을 실시하고, 1811년 12월에 거병했다. 끈질긴 항전과 인근
농민들의 지지를 바탕으로 4개월가량 버티다가 관군에 의해 진압되고 교전 중에 총
격으로 죽었다.

Hong Gyeongnae's Rebellion

Hong Gyeongnae, failing a military service test. His age is 40.

Age 40. Can a man take over a nation?

If he is a man, he may be able to subvert Joseon Dynasty,

Where however stupid they are, the people from a powerful family can pass the exam,

Where a tax regime, grain collecting, and levy of military service are in disorder, and bureaucrats exploit people

An unfair country, which uses the people from Pyeongando and Hamgyongdo in times of a national crisis and after it passes, rejects to give them a privileged positions.

Age 40. After only 5 months, he falls down shedding blood but he is joyous.

I, commander-in-chief, will open a new world.

Certainly, someone will raise a rebellion after me.

I die now, yet my dying is never dying.

Age 40. Is there anything to be desired, commander-in-chief!

---

* Hong Gyeongnae caused a farmers' revolt in 1811 to eliminate corruption in society.

순조, 붕어하다

왕권 확립을 도모하였으나 생전에 그 뜻 이루지 못하고
천주교도를 죽이고 권문세도가에게 휘둘리다
민란이 발발하여 혼돈 판국에 병들어
춘추 한창 때인 마흔다섯 해를 일기로 순조, 붕어하다

* 순조대왕 : 정조의 둘째 아들로 재위기간 동안 안동김씨 세도정권의 확립으로 국정을
  주도하지 못했으며, 봉건사회의 모순이 심화되어 대규모의 농민항쟁이 일어났다. 순
  조는 재위 34년 만에 45세의 나이로 죽었다. 능은 경기도 광주에 있는 인릉仁陵이다.

King Soonjo's Death

While not realizing a dream of establishing royal authority during his life,

And killing Catholics, swayed by the powerful families,

King Soonjo fell ill in the turmoil of revolt, and

Died at age 45 in th prime of youth.

* Soonjo : The 23th King of Joseon.

철종 즉위와 순원왕후의 수렴청정

순조의 붕어는 안동김씨 등장을 알리는 신호탄
영조의 계비 정순왕후의 전례에 따라
헌종을 옹립하고 대왕대비로 수렴청정하다
헌종이 스물셋에 죽자 일명 강화도령인 철종을 옹립,
다시 조선국을 수렴청정한 어인, 순원왕후

조선국은 이즈음 안동김씨의 조선
백성의 생사여탈권을 장악한 척신에 의하여 조선은
아이가 독사 굴에 들어가는 형국이라
개혁을 부르짖는 신흥 세력들 단번에 모조리 척살되다

추사 사후 일 년을 더 살고 예순아홉 살에 영면한
여인으로 두 왕조에 걸쳐 조선왕이 된 여인, 순원왕후

* 순원왕후(1789-1857) : 조선 순조의 비. 익종의 어머니이며, 안동김씨 영안부원군 조순
  의 딸이다.

The Accession of King Cheoljong to the Throne and the Regency by the Queen Grandmother Soonwon

Soonjo's death heralded the reign of the Andong Kim Clans
Following Queen Jeongsoon's example,
Soonwon enthroned Heonjong and acted as regent.
After Heonjong died at age 23, the queen grandmother enthroned Cheoljong
To act as regent again.

At the time of the reign of Andong Kim Clans
Which looked as if a child went into a tunnel full of poisonous snakes.
King's family who exerted the life or death authority of people
Destroyed all the new powers hoping for revolution at one time.

One year after Chusa's death, she died at age 69
Queen Soonwon, who acted as regent for 2 kings as a woman.

* Queen Soonwon : King Soonjo's wife.

등청 登廳

- 가친 김노경, 다시 판의금부사에 오르다

죄명 뒤집어씌워 내쳤다가
어명 내려
다시 판의금부사, 금관조복 입고 등청하다
대신들이 앞다퉈 인사하는 궐 안에
땡볕 칠월의 혓바닥 붉다

* 판의금부사 : 조선시대 의금부의 으뜸 벼슬인 판사로 종일품 관직으로, 흔히 금부도
  사는 이 판의 금부사를 말한다.

Office Attendance

- His Father Is Reinstated

Putting the guilt on father and rejecting

The king issued a command.

Reinstated to a head of Royal Investigation Bureau

He attends the office, wearing an official outfit.

The ministers in the palace scramble to greet

Sizzling heat of July has a red tongue

별이 뜨다
- 추사, 성균관 대사성이 되다

추론키 어려워라 추사는 당대 조선 제일의 명사,
뭇 인재들이 쉴 새 없이 성균관으로 달려가서
붓의 일생을 꿈꾸며 붓의 자리 펼 때
실눈 뜨는 별들 품어주는 초저녁 밤하늘 곱다

* 대사성 : 조선시대 성균관의 최고 전임관원으로서 정3품의 당상관직. 한 달에 두 번
  씩 성균관에서 유생들을 데리고 분향제례 하는 비교적 한직이었다.

Stars Appear

- Chusa, be a Daesaseong of Royal Academy

That Chusa was a reigning figure is anybody's guess.

When a lot of talented people ran to Seonggyungwan

And sat on dreaming of the life with a brush,

The early night sky embraces stars opening their eyes slightly.

* Seonggyungwan : Royal university to prepare the future government officials,

다산 정약용 별세하다

선량한 민초들이 공권력의 칼날 아래 살해되다
터무니없는 세금 부과와 주지육림이라는
단꿈에 빠진 나라에게 짓밟혀 나뒹구는 어린 백성들은
혹한 아니라도 장살杖殺당하기 일쑤인데
벼슬길 나섰다가 딩젱에 찢기어 상한 몸으로
서학에 옭혀 있다 겨우 배교背教로 구명求命한 대유大儒가
유배생활 어언 십팔 년여의 풍상에 시달리다
해배되었으나 곤한 몸엔 병 깊어
골수에까지 다다른 맹독에 젓 담은 육신 추슬러
이월 스무이튿날 이 험한 대지에 일흔다섯의 수壽를 끝으로
조선조 성리학의 대가이자 대 문호, 대 사상가에다
조선조 최대의 저서를 남긴 다산 선생이
처마 고드름 물 녹아 떨어지는 새벽녘에 영면하다

Dasan Jeong Yakyong, Pass Away

The good grass roots were destroyed by governmental forces.

By ruinous taxes and the nation

That was hooked on orgies, poor people were trampled,

Or they were frequently flogged to death.

In his official life, Jeong Yakyong was torn by party strife

At the expense of Catholic faith, the great Confucianist saved his life.

After 18 years in exile, unawares, full of hardships

He returned home yet had a serious disease,

Whose poison spread to the back,

Aged 75 on February 22 in this rough world

Dasan who was a great explorer in Neo Confucianism, a great man
of letters, and a great thinker, and

Who also set the record for total number of his works in Joseon,

Passed away at dawn when icicle water dropped

추사 부친의 유언

오래 배부르면 반드시 배고픈 시간이 오고
오래 부귀하면 반드시 고난의 시절을 겪나니
네 어머니가 나를 부르던 지난 밤 꿈길,
오늘 네 어머니 곁으로 가게 되면 나는 아마 다시 태어나
너와 나의 탯줄 묻힌 구렁목으로
예산 고을 신암의 삼태기 마을, 그리운 구렁목으로
살바람 타고 곧장 달려가 예산 흙 되리니
나 죽걸랑 일단 여기 나 살던 과천 땅에 깊이 묻거라
훗날 네가 아비 유택을 찾아올 것이다
자왈, 출문여견대빈出門如見大賓, 사민여승대제使民如承大祭, 이 말이[1]
내가 죽고 난 뒤에 너를 살릴 말이라
이 말을 네 심혼에 새겨 저승에서 나를 만날 때에
그 때 네 목에서 내려놓거라
실로 너는 나의 굳건한 부형이었단다, 정희야

* 『논어』의 「안연」 편에 나오는 말로, '문을 나서면 큰 손님을 대하듯 하고, 사람을 부릴
  적에는 큰 제사를 받들 듯이 하라'는 뜻이다.

Father's Will

Though he is full now, as time goes on, he must be hungry, just as
Though he is wealthy now, someday he must suffer hardship in his life.
I had a dream last night where your mother called me.
Today if I go where your mother is, maybe I will be reborn
In Gooreungmok, a basket shaped town, in Sinam of Yesan
Where your and my umbilical cords are buried,
As a dirt there, rushing on a chilly wind.
If I die, bury me deeply in Gwacheon where I used to live first.
I will visit my grave someday.
   A quotation, '出門如見大賓 使民如承大祭', meaning 'you should
treat all the people who you meet as a great guest'
Will save your life after I died
Keep it in your soul and until we meet each other in after life
Don't forget it.
Jeonghui, you are indeed my father and elder brother.

부친 김노경, 영면하다

숨이, 갑자기 숨이 막히다
천붕지탄, 하늘 무너지는 통증
캄캄하여 아무 것도 안 보이다
진달래 피어나는 봄철에
처음 붓 잡는 이치 가르쳐주시고
처음 양 볼에 입 맞춰 주시고
처음 걸음마 붙잡아 안아주시던
일흔두 살에 이른 가친이
행장 차려 길 떠나는 저승길,
길쌈 아낙들 수의 마름질하는 병풍 앞
실타래 돌려 명줄 잡아당기는
서녘 하늘 얼어붙은 눈달
예산 고택 석정물 한 모금 마시나
오석산 딸린 마른 강 지나
저승꽃술 자리 털며 가시는 영원길
갑자기 정신 혼미하여져
돌연 잃어버린 천지간의 신神,
단 한 어른, 부처를 잃고
비틀거리다 추사, 쓰러지다

Father Goes to His Final Rest

Gasp. Suddenly, I gasped

At the news of my father's death, and as though the world caved in,

With pain, I went blank and couldn't see anything.

In spring when the azalea bursted into blossom in the snow,

My father aged 72, who

For the first time, taught me how to hold the brush,

For the first time, kissed my cheeks, and

For the first time, taught step, holding me,

Went on his last journey, outfitting himself.

When woman weavers made shroud hurriedly before the folding screen,

Spinning the thread skein to pull the life strings

Is the frozen snow moon in the western sky

Does drink the water from the stone well of Yesan ?

Father goes to the road to Eternity, beating the liver spots off

Crossing the dry river beside Oseoksan

The gods of heaven and earth, who

Suddenly became delirious and expired unexpectedly

Losing only one mzee and Budda

Chusa staggers and then falls down.

목숨을 겁박하는 상소문
- 김노경 관련 윤상도 옥사 재조사를 요구하다

국왕은 겨우 열네 살, 거칠 게 없다
오도 가도 못하게 족쳐야 한다 족치다 보면 무언가 나온다
반드시 무언가 나올 것이다
김홍근이 대사헌에 오른 지 불과 열흘 만에
사직서를 써놓고 이미 십 년 전 윤상도 옥사 사건을 거론,
오래된 정적政敵인 추사를 치기 위한 상소문이 꿈틀거리다

글이여, 더러운 글의 음흉한 술수여
글, 이 더러운 생명을 갖고 산 생명을 주살하기 시작하다

추자도에 귀양 갔던 윤상도가 한양에 끌려오다
국문장에서 윤상도는 전 승지 허성이 상소를 종용했다며
허성을 끌어들여 옥에 집어넣고 나서
윤상도 자신 역시 부자간 거열형을 당하다

이미 죽은 김노경은 생전의 벼슬과 공을 추탈하라는 하교에
작위와 봉록이 결딴나는 사막의 모래바람 태풍이
조선 천지 시꺼멓게 뒤덮으며 불어 닥쳐
도도한 월성위궁의 궁주이자 형조참판인 추사가
채 방어할 겨를 없이 추사를 옭죄어 오다

The Appeal Threating Life

- Ask for the Reinvestigation on the Yoon Sangdo's Death in Prison,
  Related to Kim Nogyeong

The king aged 14 has nothing to fear.

Berate enough to be brought to a stand. Berate and something new
is revealed.

Without fail, something new will be revealed.

In only 10 days after he became Inspector General

Kim Honggeun mentioned Yoon Sangdo' death in prison of 10
years ago, with a resignation letter written

A appeal to eliminate a old political opponent Chusa wriggles.

Writing, dirty writing's mean trick

Writing, dirty life starts to kill all living things

Yoon Sangdo in exile to Chujado was summoned to Seoul

During an interrogation, he said Heo Sung urged him to appeal,

Getting Heo Sung entangled and imprisoned

Finally, he and his son were also quartered.

The king ordered that the late Kim Nogyeong's position and
contribution in his life be pulled down

The sandstorm in desert, sweeping a title and a stipend

Blew and covered the nation darkly

The owner of Wolsungwee and vice minister of Ministry of Justice, Chusa

Without protecting himself, is being strangled.

형조참판 및 동부지사에서 죄인으로 급 전락

자제 군관의 자격으로 입연한 지 삼십여 년 만이다
선친을 따라가던 그 연경 길을 동부지사가 되어 가는 감격은 크다
선친을 그리며 그 발자국을 헤아려보는 길,
허나 독수리가 서리병아리 노리는 형국인 조정에서 음모 꾸미다
양사兩司의 수장인 대사간 대사헌이 뭉쳐
이미 작고한 김노경을 탄핵하면서 음모의 과녁으로
그 정중앙에 추사를 겨냥한 불화살을 쏘아대기 시작하다
청명한 하늘 뒤덮으며 한바탕 회오리바람 몰아치다
경주김씨 일문을 향한 안동김씨의 연합전선이 효과를 거둬
추사와 아우 명희는 사관록에서 삭제되다
동지부사 일정이 취소된 채로 금호별서로 급거 퇴거,
추사, 부복하여 죄를 기다리는 중 황급히 누군가 가문을 잇게 하여
월성위궁 계자季子를 궁리하며 다시 예산 향저로 갈 때
일흔셋의 김우명이 득의에 찬 웃음 자아낸다
툇마루 시렁 줄에 실려 오는 까마귀 떼 울음은 음습하고
벼린 칼날에 전신 낭자 당하듯 추사 홀로 떨고 있다

* 양사 : 조선시대 사간원과 사헌부를 지칭.
* 금호별서 : 추사의 가친 김노경이 과천에 만들어 놓은 별장 형태의 집.

Forfeit Official Positions and Become a Criminal

30 years has passed since he went to Beijing as the son of a military official

With the late father. What a thrill it is to go there again as a Dongbugisa

The way is to retrace his steps, missing his father

Yet, the royal court like an eagle hunts for a chick conspires

The Inspector General and the Chief Censor work together

To denounce the late father Kim Nogyeong and as the target of the conspiracy

To use Chusa, starting to shoot fire arrows

A whirlwind blows, covering the clear sky

An Alliance of Andong Kim Clans against Gyeongju Kim Clans achieve effect, and

Chusa and Myonghee, his brother are deleted from the official record

With Dongbugisa's schedule canceled, he hurriedly return to Geumhobyeolseo

And then prostrates to wait for a crime. Meanwhile, to adopt a son of Wolsungwee Palace

Who will perpetuate the family line, people hastily gather in Hyangjeo in Yesan Kim Umyeong aged 73 laughs gleefully.

Cawing of crows borne on the rack strings above the toenmaru is dreary and damp

Chusa is trembling as if to be stabbed with a sharp knife all over body

허련, 예산 향저에서 한양으로 향하다

월성위궁에서 머물다 예산으로 물러난
추사를 찾아간 허련이 정중히 절 올리다
거대 정치적 음모 사슬의 올가미 걸려
천길 벼랑으로 실종되는 스승을 옆에서 섬기다
추사가 예신으로 쫓겨나자
서둘러 추사를 쫓아가는 충직한 허련은
한양에서 내려온 금부도사 오랏줄에 묶여
한여름 밤 예산에서 포박당하여 의금부로 끌려간
스승 추사를 허겁지겁 다시 뒤따라가다
고꾸라져 콧등 박살나면서도
아무런 잘못 없이 순전히 당쟁의 폭풍에 휘말린
경외하는 스승을 슬피 울며 바라보다

* 1840년 8월 20일 한밤중. 8월 초순 예산 향저에 내려온 추사는 한양에서 급거 말을 달
  려온 금부도사 박제소朴齊韶에게 포박을 당한 후에 걸어서 의금부 옥에 투옥된다. 추
  사는 김양순의 말 한 마디에 영문도 모른 채 옥에 갇히다.

Heoryeon, Go to Seoul from Hometown in Yesan

On his moving to Yesan from Wolsungwee Palace
Heoryeon visited and greeted Chusa politely,
Entangled in a vast political conspiracy,
Falling from a thousand foot cliff,
His master he sattended close to.
Also, the faithful disciple followed
Chusa, expelled to Yesan. Later on,
Tied up by Kumboodosa(procurator) from Seoul,
Taken to Uigeumbu in a mid summer night
His master he followed in a flurry,
Falling down and breaking his nose.
Innocent, involved in party strife
His respectable master he stared at, crying sorrowfully.

천안의 버선발

대감, 이 나라 조선국에서 대감보다 곧은 이 뉘이니까?
대감, 이 나라 조선국에서 대감보다 곧은 이 뉘이니까?
울며 포승줄 자락 잡고 뒤쫓아 오는 길에
버선코가 발꿈치에 있고 치마는 죄다 찢어져 버렸나이다
예산집에서 뒤쫓아 오긴 왔으나
기력이 다하여 소첩은 여기 천안에서 대감과 작별입니다
이제 어느 때에 다시 대면하리까
이승 건너 소첩이 한 번이고 열 번이고 찾아가 뵈리니
대감, 몸을 보중하소서, 부디 굳게 마음 가지소서, 대감!

Stocking Feet

Milord, who is more righteous than you in this nation?
Milord, who is more righteous than you in this nation?
On the way to walk behind you tied with rope
My stockings was taken off and my skirt torn.
As following you from home in Yesan
Run out of steam, I have to be parted from you in here, Chenan.
Now I wonder when we meet again.
To meet you, I will go several times.
Milord, take care of yourself and steel yourself!

아내와의 마지막 대화
- 추사, 천안에서 예안이씨에게 한 말

　내 말 잘 들으시오, 부인. 나는 죽지 않고 반드시 내 발로 걸어 예산 향 저, 부인 계시는 곳으로 반드시 부인을 만나러 곧 가리니 조금도 염려치 말고 부인, 아무 염려마시고 부디 연약한 옥체 보중하시라. 부인이 이 세상에 계시는 한 나는 천하태평이라, 무엇이 걱정이고 무엇이 두려우랴. 오늘 내 비록 포승에 묶어 가나 부인이 게시는 한 나는 안온하오. 부인만이 나의 평안이시오.

The Last Dialogue with Wife
- Chusa Talks to Yean Lee in Cheonan

Listen to my words, Darling. I will come back alive to you and here to my hometown on foot, so don't worry about me at all, darling. Please be healthy. As long as you live in this world, I am carefree and have nothing to fear. Although I am taken away tied up I am carefree as long as you are. Only you are my peace.

추사, 의금부 옥獄에 갇히다

누가 감히 하늘 그물망을 끊을 수 있겠는가
하늘 법도가 정연하거늘 죄 없는 이 몸을 누가 해할 것인가
추사, 앙연히 고개 들어 청천 푸른빛을 둘러보다

Chusa in Prison

Who dare to cut the mesh of heaven?

Under heaven's perfect law, nobody can do an innocent person harm.

Chusa, look at the cloudless, blue sky raising his head.

무고誣告

'이씨 성을 가진 유생이 김정희 짓이라 하였나이다'
추사가 관직에 나간 지 만 이십여 성상이 흐른
1840년 8월 23일부터 영부사를 재판장으로 시작된 추국推鞫,
윤상도 상소의 주모자로 추사를 거명한 대사헌 김양순은
추사가 이씨 성을 가진 유생과의 대질을 요청하자
다시 말을 바꿔 추국현장에서 고변하길
'이씨 성을 가진 유생은 이미 죽었나이다' 말하다
고문과 곤장으로 심문하자 김양순은 다시 말하길
'잘 생각해보니 그 이씨 성을 가진 유생은 이화면이다' 말하다
꼿꼿한 몸으로 추국 형장으로 나온 승지 허성은
태안군수 시절, 암행어사인 추사로부터 파직 상소를 당했지만
재판장 이상황의 날카로운 질문에 당당히
'과연 상소문의 수정은 본인 허성이 한 게 맞으나
이화면이 누구인지 모르고, 김정희와 관련은 없나이다' 잘라 말하다
추사가 다시 이화면과 대질을 요구하자 김양순 왈,
'이화면 역시 죽고 없으나 소신의 말이 사실입니다' 하다
그러니까 말들만 살아 움직일 뿐, 증인이 없는 이 무고,
이 근거 없는 무고에 추사 육신은 만신창이라
이 날부터 고문, 곤장이 추사를 찢어놓기 시작하다

* 추국 : 조선시대 의금부에서 임금의 특명에 따라 중죄인을 심문하던 일.
* 김양순(1776-1840) : 조선 후기의 문신.

False Accusation

One scholar with the last name Lee said, 'Kim Jeonghui did it'

In 20 years after his entrance into office

From August 23, 1840, Chusa was interrogated.

Inspector General, Kim Yangsun designated Chusa as a leader of appeal against Yoon Sangdo, and

When Chusa asked for a confrontation with the scholar,

'The one with the last name Lee died', he said

Interrogated with torture, Kim Yangsun restated,

'On second thoughts, the one with the last name Lee is Lee Hwamyeon'

Heoseong, a official in Royal Secretariat, came to the interrogation place in an upright posture,

Who was appealed discharge by Chusa, a secret royal inspector while a governor in Taeangun, yet

Searching questions by the presiding judge Lee Sanghwang

'I, Heoseong, modified the appeal,

However, I don't know who Lee Hwamyeon is, and also Kim Jeonghui was not involved', he definitely answered

Again, Chusa asked for a confrontation with Lee Hwamyeon, whereupon Kim Yangsun said,

'Lee Hyamyeon also died, yet my words are true.'

A false accusation, in which just words came to life without witnesses

By groundless false accusation, Chusa was throughly hurt

From the day on, flogging started to tear his body

추사, 고문당하며 곤장을 맞다

1840년 8월 23일, 대사헌 김양순은 한 차례의 고문과 곤장 7대를, 전 승지 허성은 한 차례의 고문과 곤장 5대, 추사는 한 차례의 고문과 곤장 5대를 맞다 김양순은 곤장의 장독杖毒으로 8월 28일 한낮에 옥중에서 비명횡사하다 전 승지 허성은 윤상도에게 상소를 올리도록 사주한 죄와 상소문을 수정한 죄로 8월 30일, 서대문 밖에서 능지처참 당하였다 살아남은 이는 오직 추사 한 사람, 풍전등화의 추사 목숨줄 거두는 거야 여반장이라 세도정치의 정적들이 호방한 술잔을 부딪치며 대취하여 양사를 동원하여 압박을 해대기 시작했다. 추사의 목숨을 노리는 무자비한 줄 상소 열기로 악마구리떼 들끓어 9월 3일에 드디어 추사의 목숨줄을 장독으로 거두려 작정하였다 추사는 이날 다시 여섯 번째의 고문을 당하고 곤장 9대를 맞았다 목숨은 겨우겨우 붙어 있으나 전신을 움직이는 일은 불가능했다. 추사는 더 이상 움직일 기력조차 없는 처참지경으로 내몰렸다 고문의 상처로 뼈와 살이 부서졌다 그날 추사의 유일한 희망은 죽음이었다 너무나 큰 고통은 강한 정신을 압도하여 의식의 무의식을 초래하였다 죽는 것이다 죽어가는 것이다 추사는 자신이 죽어가는 걸 목도하였다 자신의 시신을 보았다 힘없고 초라한 늙은이의 죽음을 아내 예안이씨만은 거둬 주리라 그녀는 내 아내는 내 아내는 내 아내는 나를 내 몸을 거둬 주리라 그리하리라 하리라…… 그러다 의식을 잃었다 어느덧 해설피 고추잠자리가 간간히 추국장의 언저리를 돌며 날던 바로 그 때, 환상인가 추사의 가녀린 목숨이 끊어지기 직전에 저 멀리에서 희미한 물안개 사이로 아내 예안이씨가 걸어오는 게 보였다 엊그제 운명하신 아버지 김노경의 얼굴이 아내의 치맛자락에 휘감겨 보였다 안 보였다 하며 같이 걸어오는 게 보였다 아, 아니 이게 어찌된 일인가 추사가 황망히 아버지에게 무슨 말인가를 하려하는 중인데 두 사람이 조금 가까이 오더니 활짝 웃다 그리고는 추사가 이내 다시 정신을 잃자 숨이 끊어졌다며 죽은 줄로 착각한 형부 관리들이 서둘러 등에 추사를 업고 달려 옥에 눕혀놓고는 자물쇠도 채우지 않고 갔다

* 추국일지를 보면 1840년 8월 23일부터 1840년 9월 3일까지, 추국장에서 추사가 고문당하며 곤장을 맞는 일자와 장면과 상황이 상세히 기술되어져 있다. 이 글은 그를 기저로 썼다.

Chusa, be Tortured and Flogged

On August 23rd, 1840, Inspector General, Kim Yangsoon suffered one torture and got 7 lashes, and the former royal secretary Heo Seong and Chusa one torture and 5 lashes. Kim Yangsoon perished because of wound poison at noon on August 28th. The former royal secretary Heo Seong was quartered outside Seodaemun with instigating and revising public appeals. Chusa was only one person who survived. As he was in critical condition, anyone could take his life easily. Political opponents laughed broadly, dead drunk and started to oppress. To kill Chusa, they lodged a series of public appeals, as a result of them, he suffered 6 tortures and got 9 lashes on September 3rd. Since he was barely alive, he couldn't keep himself steady. Chusa lacked vigor to move in horrible condition. His bone and flesh were broken by tortures and lashes. On that day, his only wish was to die. Agonies overwhelmed strong willpower, and he hovered on the edge of consciousness. He would die. He was dying. Chusa saw himself dying. He saw his dead body. His wife, Yean Lee would take a weak and poor old body by all means. She, my wife, my wife, my wife would definitely take care of my body, whatever may happen··· thinking, he passed out. At that time when a red dragonfly flied around the torturing place, was it an illusion? He saw his wife Yean Lee walking far off in the fog in the instant of his life's being extinct. He also saw his late father who came to be visible or not covered with her skirt, walking together. What happened? When he was about to talk about something to his father in a hurry, they came near to him and grinned. Chusa passed out again, and of ficials who thought he was dead laid him in the prison and left it, without locking the door.

죽음을 앞질러 보다

추사와 대질심문 중에 김양순이 장살杖殺 당하다
거명된 승지 허성은 능지처참 당하고
천길 벼랑 아래 흉포한 개죽음 물살 드세어
국문을 기다리는 단 한 명의 죄인 추사 역시 장살될 위기다
이렇게 한평생이 마감되는구나
진창에 빠져 오도 가도 못하고 몽둥이 맞아 죽게 된
추사, 하릴없이 죽는 자신의 죽음을 앞질러 보다

See His Dead Body Beforehand

During a cross examination with Chusa, Kim Yangsoon was flogged to death.

The former royal secretary Heo Seong named was quartered.

Anyone in the strong current under the thousand foot cliff would die in vain.

Only one prisoner, Chusa was on the brink of being flogged to death, waiting for being questioned.

'Like this, I will finish my life'

Flogged to death, stuck deep in the mud and stalled

Chusa, see himself die in vain beforehand

한여름철 여명의 통곡

내 정신 한 켠 졸졸졸 맑은 물 한 줄기 흐르고 있다
그러나 자세히 보라 그것이 물인가? 나의 피다
나의 피가 아니라 내 처참한 심중의 울음, 내 슬픈 죽음이다
새벽녘 내내 정신 몽롱하다 괴로운 밤이 가고 있다
날 새면 나무 몽둥이기 내 혼 될 거라
부처의 열반이 이리 급박하게 오고 나는 이미 죽어 있다
나는 시체다 나는 이름을 상실한 시체다 그토록
내 그토록 고대한 새 예술의 개척은 한낱 뜬구름의 몽환, 시체다
일신 욕보이고 멸문지경에 이르렀으니
산다 하여 사내, 어찌 이에 이르러 고개 들고 살아갈 것인가
무죄 항변한들 포악한 독거미가 가납할 것인가
오호라 한 생의 필멸을 마다할 수 없는 일, 가마 고요히 가주마
푹푹 찌는 팔월 한여름철 여명이다 고통의 새벽이다
오라, 자, 육신 찢어먹을 승냥이들아 오거라
내 영혼만큼은 자유다 오라 지체치 말고 어서 오라

The Wail of Midsummer Dawn

A brook trickling is in my mind.

However, look at it closely. Water? It's my blood.

No. It's not my blood but my tears and my sorrowful death.

The night during which I felt woozy is passing

After the dawn breaks, I will be beaten to a soul by a club.

Buddha's nirvana is coming urgently, and I am already dead.

I am a corpse. A corpse that lost its name. My earnest,

Earnest hope to open the new arts became a transient dream, a corpse.

Disgracing myself at the end of the extermination of a whole family

Though escaping death, how can a man live lead a blameless life?

Certainly, it has become evident that the tyrannical lycosids will not
appreciate my protestation of innocence.

Alas, life is subject to decay. I will go. I will go without a word.

A sultry summer day in August is breaking.

Come, dhole. Come to tear up my body.

Yet, my soul is free. Don't hesitate to come to me!

기적적인 죽음에의 탈출

조정의 대소신료들은 추사의 장살을 점치다
누구 한 사람 추사의 국문장鞠問場 장살을 의심하는 이 없다
옴짝달싹 할 수 없는 장살 주문이 쇄도하여
형방 포졸들이 나무 몽둥이 다잡고 있는 터,
대책 없는 상황선개 믹을 그 어떤 방도를 못 찾다
그야말로 절체절명의 상황에서 막역한 벗 우의정이 상소 올리다
젊은 시절 함께 금석문을 연구하고
학예의 도반이자 친구로서 당시 우의정 조인영은
간결하나 논리 정연히 항변 못할 조항을 들어
추사 죄는 죽어 마땅하나 대질할 증인들이 모두 죽었음을 들어
차자箚子, 곧 죽음에서 감 일등하자는 상소로 추사, 감사減死되다
양사兩司가 벌떼처럼 추사의 국문을 요구했으나
당시 수렴청정을 하는 대왕대비는 재차
'김정희를 대정현에 위리안치하라' 명하다
목숨이 끊어지기 직전에 기적적으로 되살아난
추사 목숨 부지는 조인영의 도움이지만
뉘 아는가, 하늘 그물망 운행은 정연한 것을

* 대정현 : 제주특별자치도 서귀포시 중심부 서쪽과 대정읍·안덕면 일대에 있었던 옛 고
  을 이름.
* 감사減死 : 사형을 내려야 하나 감사, 즉, 사死할 죄명을 한 단계 낮춰 죽임을 면하게 하다.

A Miraculous Escape from Death

All courtiers in Royal Court predicted Chusa would be beaten to death.

Anyone didn't doubt his death by flogging in the interrogation place

The petition for having him killed by flogging poured in, with his hand and foot bound, and

The pojols of Ministry of Justice waited, holding a wooden club tightly.

There was no means of dealing with a hopeless quandary

In a desperately dangerous situation, his intimate friend and Right State Councillor in one appealed,

Who had studied an epigraph together in early life and

Whose name was Jo Inyeong, his boon companion in studying arts and science

His appeal was so simple and perfectly logical clause by clause as to be unanswerable

Chusa deserved to die, yet there was no witness to confront with each other

Hence, a reduced penalty should be given, said the appeal, which made him escape from death

On this, the Offices of Inspector General and of Censor like bees asked for interrogation with torture.

Then the Queen Dowager, a regent again

Condemned him to exile to Daejung-hyun

Thanks to Jo Inyeong,

Chusa escaped death by a miracle. However,

Who knew? How orderly and logical the providence of Heaven is

* pojols : policemen

제4장

조선의 씨눈

추사의 제주도 유배, 북청 유배에서 죽음까지

The Embryo of Joseon

Chusa's Exile to Jeju Island and Bookcheong and His Death

조선의 씨눈

거세게 부는 구월 칼바람,
매정하다 이 땅의 피비린내여
눈물 흘릴 여가 없이 내몰린 한데에서 나는
내 냉가슴 두드려 나를 품다
내 속에서 오래전 발아 시작한 어둠이
간 봄에 이미 싹을 틔웠으므로
울부짖어 외쳐댈 고적한 함성들의 나라를 향하여
가을 겨울이여 고백하마, 나는
스러지는 목숨이 아니다, 나는
고꾸라지는 목숨이 아니다, 나는
죽어 사라지는 목숨이 아니다, 살아서 나는
알몸으로 알몸 태우는 살맛의 세상,
동지섣달 허공에 푸르른
푸르른 몸 뻗는 조선 참나무 겨우살이다
별빛 찬란한 조선의 씨눈이다

The Embryo of Joseon

September. The blood wind blows hard.

Heartless, bloody on the ground.

Without having time to shed tears, driven out of the house

I, suffering in silence, embrace myself.

The darkness that started to germinate in melong since

Already sprouted last spring.

Hence, facing the solitary nation of shouts, wailing

Fall and winter, I will confess, I

Will never collapse, I

Will never fall prone, and I

Will never die and disappear, and alive

In the world, broiling, naked

I will be a taxillus yadoriki

Spreading branches into the air in hard winter.

I am the brilliant embryo of Joseon.

형제의 다른 이름, 초의선사

전주를 거쳐 제주도 가는 길목
해남 대둔사에 이르러 추사는 일지암을 찾다
일찍이 서산대사가 종법 전하며
'만세토록 허물어지지 않을 땅이며 종통이 돌아갈 곳'이라
명명한 해남 두륜산 숲속 암자는 초의선사 거처,
유배 중에도 추사, 풍류 넘쳐나
지필 꺼내들고는 대둔사 '무량수각' 현판을 쓰다
상한 몸 대신 혼이 쓰는 붓몸을
초의는 껄껄 웃으며 그윽이 바라보다
그 눈길 따라 뱃길 건너 제주로
훗날 추사 찾아와 유배지에서 반년을 머문
초의선사와 나눈 가을밤의 정분

Choui Seonsa, Another Name for Brother

On the way to Jeju Island traveling through Jeonju

Chusa visited Iljiam of Daedunsa

Which was a Duryunsan hermitage in Haenam and Choui Seonsa's abode,

To which Suhsan Daisa who early spread the religious rules, referred,

As the place 'that will be home to Buddhist scriptures, not torn down forever'.

While in exile, full of appreciation for the arts

He took out paper and brush and wrote a signboard of Daedunsa reading 'Muryangsugak',

With his spirit, not his injured body

Meanwhile, Choui Seonsa looked at him silently.

His look led to Jeju over the sea later on, and

Choui Seonsa stayed with Chusa in exile for half a year.

Their affection in the autumn night.

바람을 타다

곤장에 갈라진 몸에서 바람이 불다
거룻뱃머리 뒤흔들며 심히 미약한 맥박 치며 불다
폭풍 휘몰아치는 한가운데에 파도,
금방이라도 거룻배 삼킬 듯 휘몰아치다
제수 바다 고기밥으로 숙어간 제수 사내들 혼령이여 오시라
줄 끊긴 거문고 타듯이 바람을 타다
제주조랑말 올라타듯이 바람에 올라타는
나는 추사다, 제주 바다 폭풍이여 내 붓으로 노를 저어
나를 제물로 바다 가르라, 나는 추사,
오래전 이미 죽은 주검이 어찌 나를 근심케 하랴
바람을 타는 조선 사내, 나는 추사다

* 추사가 제주 바다를 건너던 때의 정황을 편지로 써서 아우 명희에게 보낸 편지글에
  서 인용.

Ride the Wind

The wind blows in through the torn body by flogging.

It blows beating the weak pulse as the bow of the boat shakes

The violent storm in the sea blows, and the wind

Is likely to swallow the boat any moment.

Spirits of the dead men, who became fish food in Jeju sea, come.

As if to paly the geomungo with broken strings, I ride the wind.

As if to ride a pony, riding the wind,

I am Chusa. Jeju sea of storms, row by using my brush

Devide the sea, victimizing me, Chusa.

How dare does a long dead person make me worry?

Joseon man who can ride a wind, I am Chusa.

* A quotation from the letter to his brother Myeonghui about sailing cross the sea.

이진포에서 거룻배 타고 제주도로

더러 해남의 이진포에서 제주까지
보따리 맨 하인 봉이의 손잡다
삭탈관직에다 추국고문에 상한 몸 이끌고
돛대에 의지하여
바다 갈매기들조차 날기 힘든 제주 땅,
알 수 없는 운명의 격랑을 마시며
낙엽보다 가벼운 늙은이로
낡은 거룻배에 실려 타두에 앉자
예산의 예안이씨의 마음도 화북진에 닿다

* 타두 : 배의 방향을 잡는 기구. 배의 키를 말한다.
* 화북진 : 지금의 제주시 화북동인 화북진은 현에서 10리 떨어진 항구로 추사에 앞서
  우암 송시열이 들어왔고, 추사 이후로는 면암 최익현이 유배왔다.

From Ijinpo to Jeju Island by Barge

Traveling from Ijinpo in Haenam to Jeju

He sometimes held Bonghee's hand.

Removed from office, and interrogated with tortures

Chusa, weak, leaned against the mast.

Jeju was the difficult place for even sea gulls to reach.

Swept in great seas of unknowable fate

By the time an old man as light as a fallen leave

Got on an old boat and sat at the helm,

Yean Lee's heart in Yesan reached Hwabukjin.

제주에서의 첫날 밤

추사가 제주에 온 첫날 물허벅 등에 진 종종걸음 제주 여인들이 초가에 들었다 제주 해녀는 망사리를 메고 오갔다 이진포에서 만난 고한익이 말하길 집 안팎의 가사와 육아 및 밭일을 하며 물허벅 등에 지고 제주 바람에 맞서 자갈투성이 길을 걸어 살아오는 이들이 제주 여인이라 했다 또 제주 해녀들은 살아서 이미 칠성판 걸머지고 창망한 바다를 생업으로 제주 바닷가 현무암 닮은 생명을 담보로 물질한다 했다 제주 여인들이 살아가는 한 세대가 척박한 바람의 땅, 제주에서의 일생의 일대기이자 제주도 바람과 해녀들의 일대기라 했다. 생소하고 낯선 풍경을 접하며 추사는 거룻배에서 내려 제주 땅 밟자 더 이상 피멍든 육신을 가눌 수 없을 정도로 피곤하였다 구월 스무이렛날 아침에 배에 올라 석양 무렵에 화북진 아래에 도착하여 그날 밤 민가에서 곤한 몸 뉘었으나 오히려 정신이 맑아지는 것은 웬일인가 그렇게 추사는 제주 첫날의 밤을 지새우다

* 고한익 : 유배 죄인인 추사를 인계받기 위하여 파송한 제주관아의 아전.

The First Day in Jeju

It was the first day Chusa came in Jeju. Setting a water jar on the back, Jeju women came into the thatched house, walking with hurried steps. They carried the net pocket on the shoulder. Ko Hanik, who met on Ijinpo said, Jeju women take care of all the household affairs as well as infant care and farm work both outside and inside the home, and their life is like walking on the gravel road against the wind, setting water jar on the back. Also, Jeju woman divers go underwater at the risk of their lives, as if to carry the bottom lining board of a coffin on their shoulder. Jeju women's life is the one on the barren and windy land and for the wind and women divers. When learning about unfamiliar sights, Chusa arrived in Jeju by barge, he felt so tired as not to keep his balance. In the morning of September 27th, he embarked in a boat and reached Hwabukjin at around sunset. That night he stayed in a private house. Though he felt tired, somehow, his mind cleared more and more. Hence, he had to stay up all first night in Cheju Island.

둘째 날, 고한익의 집에 머물다

한양 도성과 멀어질수록 삶이 한결 수월하다
화북포구에서 제주성까지 십리를 걸어
추국 형장 곤장의 피들이 예까지 왔나
냅다 하늘 흐리더니 바람 거세어진 제주성을 뒤흔드는데
갑자기 흥 돋아 봉이야, 지필묵 이리 주거라
시 한 수 짓고는 제주의 이틀째 밤부터
거룻배에서 만난 제주 아전衙前 고한익 집에 이틀간 유숙하다
사흘째 아침에 가족들 울 밖에까지 나와 인사하는
풍경에 추사, 오래만에 미소 짓다
거듭 환대에 예 갖춰 인사하고는
금오랑金吾郞 앞세워 총총 대정현으로 길 떠나다

* 봉이 : 추사 제주유배 시 맨 처음 딸려 수종을 들어준 종의 이름.
* 금오랑 : 조선시대 의금부에 딸린 도사를 달리 이르던 말. 이때 추사를 호송해간 금
  오랑은 안종식이다.

The Second Day, Stay at Go Hanik's House

The farther away from Seoul it is, the simpler life is.

Did the blood interrogation come here,

Walking 10 ri from Hwabuk port to Jeju wall?

Suddenly, it became cloudy and the violent wind blew, shaking Jeju wall.

Unexpectedly, Chusa shouted, in the mood for composing a poem,

'Bong, bring paper, brush and Korean ink.' Later, from the second day in Jeju

He stayed at Go Hanik's house for 2 days; He met a petty official, Go in a barge.

On the third morning, his family came out to see him off, Chusa smiled after a long time.

Many thanks for their hospitality, conforming to etiquette, and

He followed Geumorang hurriedly for Daejunghyun

* ri : measure the distance unit, about 4km.

대정읍성 송계순 집에서 시작한 위리안치

제주성에서 대정까지는 구십리 길,
무수천을 타고 금물덕과 시모악을 돌아
가을 단풍 물든 바굼지오름의 중산길을 굽이돌아
대정현 대정읍성 안동네에 이르다
일행 중에 정군鄭君이라 부르는 젊은이가 먼저
군교軍校인 송계순宋啓純을 만나 집을 얻다
추사는 송계순을 "주인 또한 매우 순박하고 좋다" [1] 평하며
서둘러 가시울타리 둘러 집 바깥채를 유배처로 삼다
이런 정황을 아우 명희에게 편지 쓰며
이마에 땀 훔치는 추사의 오른손 소매 깃 사이로
엄마 품에 안긴 아이 숨소리 들리다

---

* 무수천, 금물덕, 시모악 : 제주성에서 대정현까지 가는 길목으로, 해안선 길이 아닌 숲이 무성한 중산간으로 이어진 길.
* 바굼지오름 : 제주도 서귀포시에 있는 오름으로. 바굼지는 제주도 방언으로 바구니라는 뜻이며 오래전 이 일대가 바닷물에 잠겼을 때 바구니만큼만 보였다는 전설이 전해진다. 이 오름의 기슭에 대정향교가 있고, 훗날 이 향교의 현판 〈의문당疑問堂〉을 추사가 썼다.
1) 『완당선생전집』 권2에서 인용.

Start Exile Life at Song Gyesun's House in Daejeong

90 ri long from Jeju wall to Daejeong

After floating down Musucheon, go along Geummuldeok and Simoak, then

Follow winding Zhongshan Path of Bagumji Oreum covered with autumn leaves, and

Finally reach inside Daejeong

A young man of my party, called Jeonggun first

Rent official Song Gyesun's house

Chusa says "he is pure and good", and

Threw together a thorn fence and placed the outhouse as his house of exile

Writing down his situation in a letter to his brother Myeonghui

When he wiped the sweat from his forehead, from his right sleeves

The infant's breath in mom's bosom was heard.

* Oreum : Jeju dialect meaning a mountain.

새로운 경전

약관의 시절에 대망이 인도한 청나라 연경에서
스승 옹방강과 완원을 만났다
대과급제 이후 이십여 년에 벼슬이 형조참판에 이르러
혹독한 고문과 곤장 맞아 반 주검 되다
삭탈관직으로 모자라 위리안치의 생총生塚이라
선조들이 피땀으로 이룬 가업 잃고
낯설고 물 설은 독풍의 궁도窮島에 내몰렸으니 잠이 오랴
'너는 삼가 숭앙을 새기라'
황망하여라 어디선가 선친의 음성 또렷하다
분명하다 '출문여견대빈出門如見大賓' 말씀,
추사, 엎드려 숭앙崇仰의 전각篆刻을 심중에 새기다

* 궁도 : 추사는 제주섬을 궁도라 이르곤 하였다. 몸이 외롭고 정신이 괴로운데다 심혼
  이 갈급하였음을 표현한 말이다.
* 숭앙: 추사는 자신의 적거지를 찾아와 배움을 청하는 제주 사람들을 오로지 숭앙으로
  대하였다. 숭앙은 곧 추사 인격의 핵심을 이루는 주요 인자다.

A New Scripture

At the age of 20, in a long awaited Beijing of Qing China
Master Weng Fanggang and Ruan Yuan he met
In 20 years after passing the state test, when he became a vice minister
By gruesome tortures and flogging, he was half killed.
Exiled as if to be in the grave alive , not to mention removed from office
Deprived of his family's property and achievement,
How could he sleep, driven into extremely poor, unfamiliar island
with intense winds?
"Respectfully bear the deep reverence in mind."
It was embarrassing that he thought he heard his father clearly,
Saying, '出門如見大賓Chulmoonyeogeondaebin'
Prostrating himself, he carved his deep reverence for people in mind

상무商懋를 양자 삼다

위태하여라 수천 리 밖 외로이 뒹구는 목숨줄
후사後嗣, 기둥 하나 없다면야 어이 조상을 대하랴
예순 바라보는 곱다란 명주 주름 진 아내는 근래 병 깊어
아내, 예안이씨를 봉양하는 자식이자
대대손손 이어져오고 이어가야 할 가문을 지키며
월성위궁 보살펴 갈 혈육을 물색하다 추사는
지치고 상한 기력 일으켜 조카인 상무를 양자 삼다

* 추사는 제주도에 유배 온 이듬해(56세)인 1841년에 김일주의 증손자이자 추사와는 13
  촌지간인 먼 조카뻘 되는 김상무를 양자 입적시키다.

212

Adopt Sangmoo as his Heir

At stake is my life, weltering all alone thousands of ri away.

How can I meet my ancestors without leaving offspring?

My wife, pushing 60, with a lovely wrinkled face had a serious disease recently.

Chusa, looking for a person who was able to

Support his wife, Yean Lee,

Retain his family generation after generation and

take care of Wolsungwee Palace

Finally adopted cousin Sangmoo as his heir, barely recovering his strength.

진장陳醬, 그리고 행간의 풍요

- 장醬도 진장을 사서 보내라 그것도 변변치 않은 진장은 보내도 소용없
 다.' 즉, 최상품의 좋은 음식을 보내지 않으면 유배지일지언정 먹지 않
 겠다, 떼쓰면서 '민어를 사서 보내라, 겨자를 맛난 것으로 보내라, 어
 란魚卵도 먹을 만한 것을 구하여 보내라[1]

언제 사약이 내려올지 모르는 시간들인데
예산에서 대정까지 수천 리 길 등짐 지고 수행한
머슴 이름만 문헌 기록상으로 열한 명,
장도 하필 진장이요
민어도 최상품 민어에 최상품 겨자와 어란,
일류만 고집하는 이 말 속엔
한숨짓는 게딱지 초가집이 없다 목숨 걸고
온갖 세금에 혼 빠져 야반도주하는 백성들 없다
절친한 벗 조인영이 영의정 된 탓인가
행간 행간에 풍요가 깃든 이 가상의 세계!

---

1) 신축년(1841) 유월에 예산의 향저, 예안이씨에게 보낸 편지문에서 발췌.
 * 진장 : 검은콩으로 쑨 메주로 담가서 까만빛을 띠는 간장.

Thick Soy and
the Composure on the Brink of Disaster

- 'Send me thick soy of all soy. It is no use to send the humble thick soy'.
  Namely, even though he was in exile, he wanted to have the food of
  the best quality, asking for the tough things like 'send croakers, buy
  tasty mustard, and look for roe suitable to my taste'.

Even in such a situation that an official could bring poison any time
Carrying loads on the back to Daejeong situated thousands of ri
away from Yesan
The number of the servants was 11 according to references.
Thick soy of all soy, and
Only a croaker, mustard and roe of the best quality
He stuck to, yet because of his persistence,
People didn't sigh in a tiny thatched cottage, and at the risk of their life
Didn't do a moonlight flit to avoid oppressive taxes.
Was that because of his bosom friend, Jo Inyeong?
The mellow unrealistic world on the brink of disaster!

손청거리
- 대정현 강도순의 집으로 적거지를 옮기다

이태 동안 머문 두 거리 규모의 송계순 집을 떠나
제주도 전통의 신구간 동안에 강도순 집으로 거처를 옮기다
네거리 집인 이 집을 내방객들은 수성초당이라 하다

* 손청거리 : 손님맞이 사랑방.
* 신구간 : 제주도 전통의 이사 기간으로 매년 대한 후 5일부터 입춘立春전 3일까지의
  약 1주일.
* 수성초당 : 수성壽星은 인간의 수명을 관장하는 별로, 제주도 사람들은 추사 적거지를
  이름하여 수성초당이라 불렀다.

The Guest Room

- Move to Gang Dosoon's as a House of Exile

Leaving from Song Gyesoon's small scaled house where he had lived for 2 years

He moved to Gang Dosoon's during a traditional moving period.

They called the larger scaled house Suseong Chodang

염려의 장막

- 임인년(1842) 시월 초사흘, 추사의 편지

- … 갑쇠를 바꾸어 보내고 이 때부터 묵은해를 보내고는 아쉬운 일이 많
  아서 경득이를 도로 보내옵니다마는 염려가 무궁합니다. 임인년(1842)
  시월 초사흘 [1]

하인들이 예산과 제주를 오가길 수십 차례,
허나 뉘 알았으랴,
'염려가 무궁하다'는 이 말 뜻에는
시월 초사흘 추사 편지에서
아내의 병세 걱정하는 지아비의 불길한 느낌 들다
공연히 흥분되고 초조해지는
불안하고 막막한 영육 간 떨림,
왜 가까이서 멀리서 검은 장막 펄럭이는가

1) 예안이씨는 결국 추사가 보낸 이 편지를 받아보지 못하고 운명하다.

Anxiety Curtain
- Chusa's Letter of October 4, 1842

- ⋯ After I sent you another servant, Gapssoe, I saw the old year out,
  yet there left much to be desired and I sent Gyeongdeuk again. I felt
  extremely apprehensive for your safety. October 4, 1842 by the lunar
  calendar.

Dozens of times servants came and went between Yesan and Jeju Island,
Yet, who knew?
The wording, 'Worries are endless'
In his letter of October 4
Showed Chusa worried about wife's disease.
The vibration of soul and body which is restless and gloomy
Unnecessarily excited and fretful
Why is the dark curtain flapping from close and from far away?

* Yean Lee died without receiving this letter.

예안이씨의 부음

버선발로 예산에서 천안까지 형구形軀를 뒤따르며
가녀린 몸 지쳐 쓰러져 일어나길 반복하며 울던 아내가
내 곁을 떠날 줄 아니, 먼저 세상을 뜰 줄
꿈엔들, 어찌 꿈엔들 짐작이나 하였으랴
막막하고 아득하여라 천지가 사라지고 내가 사라지고 있다
통곡으로 쓴 애서문이 무슨 소용이란 말인가
부모 잃고 아내마저 세상 뜨면 더 이상의 나는 없다
내가 없으니 이름도 없다 누구도 나의 이름을 부르지 마라
아내의 죽음은 남편의 죄, 내 죄는 치유불능,

* 임인년(1842) 11월 13일 정사丁巳에 예산의 묘막墓幕에서 부인이 임종했으나, 부고는 다음달 15일 저녁에야 비로소 바다 건너에 전해져 남편 김정희는 상복을 갖추고 슬피 통곡한다. 살아서 헤어지고 죽음으로 갈라진 것을 슬퍼하고 영원히 간 길을 쫓을 수 없음이 뼈에 사무쳐서, 몇 줄 글을 엮어 집으로 보내다.

Hear of Yean Lee's Death

Following me in stocking feet from Yesan to Cheonan,
The wife of a slender frame collapsed repeatedly, crying
How did I imagine
She would leave me, what's more she predeceased me?
I am gloomy and at a loss. Heaven and earth is disappearing. So am I.
What good is the love letter filled with wailing?
As I lose even you as well as parents, I'm no longer in existence.
Without me, there is no name. Don't call my name any more.
My wife's death is ascribable to my fault, and my fault is incurable.

머슴 봉이

민망혀유 가마솥에 끓인 누룽밥 덜 불었남유
워치기 요기라도 허서야쟎유
아예 곡기 끊으실 요량은 아니시지유
대감마님, 워떡헌대유
여기 민경面鏡유 눈자위가 퉁퉁 부어오르셨유
눈이 숫제 읎어졌슈
제주는 돌땅이구먼유 아주 멀리 가서 물 한 짐 퍼 왔슈
갱싱이 정주간 작은 물항아리 채웠슈
시원하게 세수라도 허서야쟎유
크게 맘 상허지 마셔유
살아남으셔야, 끝까지 살아남으셔야
고게 강한 거 아닌감유
고게 진짜 우덜 예산의 힘이쟎유
워떡게든 살으실뀨 살어서서 그여 가실거유

Farmhand Bonghee

Sorry to give you the boiled rice swollen in a caldron.

Please stave off your hunger with it.

Aren't you going to give up some food, hey?

Milord, what can I do for you?

Look at this hand mirror. The part of your eyeball swells up, and

Your eyes have disappeared.

Jeju is full of stones and I had to go far away to get water

I barely managed to fill the water pot in the kitchen.

Why don't you wash your face to cool off, hey?

Don't get upset.

Survive, survive to the last, and

That is strong, isn't it? Yeah?

That is the power of Yesan, isn't it? Yeah?

I am sure you'll survive at any cost and go back home.

뱃사람 양봉신

아무런 대가 없이
수천 리 밖
충청도 강경에서
제주 대정마을 오가며
추사 심부름에다
일용품을 공수해 준
뱃사람 양봉신
아무런 대가 없이
추사를 섬긴 이,
아름다워라
귀한 마음행적이여

Sailor Yang Bongsin

For nothing

Coming and going to Jeju

Thousands of ri away

From Gangkyung in Chungcheongdo,

Yang Bongsin, a sailor,

Ran errands and

Provided the necessities for Chusa.

For nothing

The person who served Chusa.

What a beautiful mind

He had!

추사, 병고에 시달리다

하루하루가 결전의 날이다
우선 당장 음용할 물이 문제다
마실 물이 부족하다 길어오는 물로는
겨우 밥물 붓는 걸로 족한 상태다
거추장스러운 몸은 반 귀신이라
온몸 곳곳이 몹시 가렵고
몸 곳곳 어디 성한 데 없이 아프다
하필 콧속에 혹이 났다
온통 입 속 헤집어 음식 삼키지 못하고
팔 다리 쑤셔 기력 쇠진하다
손목 팔목 저려 붓을 잡지 못하다
더구나 시야를 가린 안질에
혹여 제주에서 죽을지라도
나는 싸움을 포기하지 않겠다

Chusa, Suffer from Illness

Every day is a battle.

Above all, to get drinking water is a hard row to hoe.

There is not enough water to drink. With the water drawn

I narrowly cook rice.

My weak body is dying, and then

I feel itchy all over, and

I feel pain all over.

I have a lump in my nose of all places and

A cold sore makes it hard for me to swallow food.

From lack of vigor, limbs are aching, and

Aching limbs discourage me from holding a brush.

Also eye illness blocks my view,

Yet, although I die in Jeju,

Never will I give up fighting.

안질眼疾

조선 국왕은 추사 제자인 허련에게 추사 안부를 묻다
왕을 백성의 어버이라며 감읍하기는 추사도 여일하여
글씨를 달라는 말에 추사 더 울어, 안질 덧치다
모슬포에서 제주 흰꼬리수리가 사체로 뜨던 겨울 아침,
추사, 진적력구眞積力久라, 그저 혼자 말하며
유배삭풍에 마모된 노구 일으켜 붓 잡아주는
제주 밤바다 거친 풍랑이 늙고 병든 추사를 바라보다

* 진적력구 : '진정성이 쌓이면 그 힘이 오래 간다'는 뜻.

228

Sore Eyes

Joseon king asked Heoryeon after Chusa.

Chusa, thinking of the king as his parents, was touched and moreover,

Hearing that the king wanted his calligraphy, wept so much that sore eyes were infected.

One winter morning, a white-tailed sea eagle floated dead at Moseulpo in Jeju.

"As time goes by, the power of truth lasts long", he murmured and

Held a blush forgetting his old age, tired of banishment and the north wind of winter.

Winds and wild waves on Jeju night sea stared at old and weak Chusa.

제주목사 장인식

- 명성이 매우 가까우니 비록 당장 손을 잡고 즐기지는 못하나마 의지와
  믿음을 지닌 것 같아서 마음 든든하오… (생략) … 보내준 여러 물품은
  특별히 정념을 쏟아 싸늘한 주방에 따스한 기가 돌게 하였소… [1]

새로 부임한 제주목사 겸 방어사는
제주도에 도착하자마자 맨 먼저 존경하는 추사를 찾다
유배객의 일용품은 해당 지역 관청의 몫,
고기, 술, 약과, 찹쌀, 해산물에다 갖가지 옷까지
제주목사 장인식은 추사를 섬겼다
그로 하여 유배 온 지 9년째 되던 해의 삼월부터
해배되는 동짓달에 이르도록 추사 평안하다

---

1) 『완당선생전집』권4, 장인식에게 보낸 서신 중.

Jeju Magistrate Jang Insik

- Though the reputation to attract attention did not make me welcome
  you, embracing you in joy, your will and trust gave me reassurance
  ⋯ The various commodity you sent, bearing emotions, brought my
  chilly kitchen alive and warmer.

A newly appointed magistrate
On arriving in Jeju, visited Chusa he worshiped.
As authorities concerned covered the necessities for exiled people
Such as meat, drink, medicine, rice, seafood, and various clothes,
Jeju magistrate Jang Insik served Chusa.
Hence, from March in 9 years after his exile
To September when his exile was released, he was peaceful.

추사의 예감

유배생활이 풀릴 것이라
막내 동생에게 봄 편지를 보낸
그해 겨울, 방송放送의 왕명이 내리다.

* 헌종 6년(1840) 9월 2일, 추사가 55세 되던 해에 제주 대정에 위리안치 하라는 왕명으
  로 제주도 유배생활을 시작한 후, 헌종14년(1848) 12월 6일 마침내 해배 왕명이 떨어진
  다. 55세에서 63세까지만으로는 8년 3개월만이다.

Chusa's Prediction

Exile curled up would be unwound

Said the letter sent to his youngest brother

That winter, his exile was finished by royal command

* Chusa was exiled to Jeju Island from 55 to 63 years old.

제주도 위리안치에서 해배되어 예산에 가다

채 안질이 낫지 않은 눈에 눈물 그렁그렁하다
제주목사가 강상에 쫓아와 보인 눈물
오로지 숭앙崇仰으로만 기른
제주 각처에서 모인 수천의 제자들 눈물이
추사와 함께 예산 선영에 절 올릴 때
바람, 조선 바람은 미친듯 설레어라
꿈에 그리던 부모님과 아내가 선히 보이고
피붙이들 일시에 모두 흐느끼다
그를 알아듣고 예산 백송도 뒤따라 크게 울다

Go to Yesan after Released from Exile

Tears stood in Chusa's sore eyes.

Jeju magistrate followed up to the riverbank and wept.

Educated only with respect

Thousand of disciples from around the nation wept

When Chusa along with them bowed low to his ancestors' graves.

Wind, Joseon's winds were bursting with joy

Parents and wife in his dreams were fresh in his memory.

All his family wept all at once, and

Recognizing him, Yesan white pine also cried loudly.

삼호에 집을 마련하다

꿈결인 듯해라 자유의 몸으로
예산 향저에 몸을 쉰 다음에 추사는
제주에서 풀려난 이듬해 봄무렵,
한강변 삼호에 몸 뉘일 작은 거처를 마련하다
수중에 재물은 없으나
자유가 있었고 주변에 추사에 헌신하는
제자들이 있는데다
칠십이구초당, 일휴정이라는 정자가 있어
몹시 곤궁한 살림살이나마
시 짓고 글 쓰는데 막힘 없다

* 칠십이구초당 : 추사의 호
* 일휴정 : 현재의 용산에 있던 정자의 이름이다. 추사는 이 일휴정과 마포와 과천 등
  지에서 노후를 보냈으나 생활은 몹시 곤궁하여 제자들이 보내주는 물품으로 겨우
  연명하다.

Get a House in Samho

To get free was like a dream.

After taking a rest in hometown in Yesan, Chusa

On around next spring after returning from exile on Jeju Island

Got a little house at Samho of the riverside of the Han-gang

Although he had no money in his hand

He was free and

Had the devoted disciples.

In addition, there was a gazebo called Ilhujung

Though Living in needy circumstances

Where he could write a poem and a essay freely.

* Ilhujung was in the current Yongsan.

이하응에게 난 그림을 교습하다

제자를 자청하는 사람
추사, 난 그리기를 가르쳐
난보蘭普인 난맹첩을 준 사람
추사 사후에
흥선대원군이 된 이하응이다

* 이하응 : 고종의 아버지가 되어 조선의 실권을 장악한 흥선대원군이다.
* 난보 : 난 그림이 그려진 화첩.

Teach How to Draw Orchids to Lee Haeung

The man who volunteered for a pupil,

To Whom Chusa taught how to draw orchids

And presented an orchid picture book later

After Chusa's death

The man, Lee Haeung became Heungseon Daewongun

* Lee Haeung : The father of Gojong, 26th King of Joseon,

추사, 함경도 북청으로 유배당하다

일명 강화도령인 철종은 열아홉 살의 나무꾼인데다가
승하한 헌종의 아저씨뻘 되는 촌수라
진종의 위패문제로 당시 영의정 권돈인과 맞서던 세도권력은
권돈인을 낭천현에 중도부처하고 그의 절친한 벗,
추사를 다시 옭아 황무지의 땅, 북청유배의 명이 내렸다
장탄식도 함관령을 넘어 변방 골짜기 험지로 유배가다

* 진종의 위패사건: 제주도에서 풀려난 지 3년 후인 1851년에는 진종의 조천 문제로
  또 한 차례 예송이 조정을 뒤흔들어 친구이자 영의정이었던 권돈인과 유배 길에 오
  르게 되었다.

Chusa, Exiled to Bukcheong in Hamgyeongdo

Cheoljong called Ganghwa lad was a 19 year old woodcutter and
Late Heonjong's uncle in the family tree.
The powers that combatted against prime minister for an ancestral tablet
Forced Kwan Donin into exile to Nangchenhyun and entrapped
His bosom friend, Chusa to drive him into exile to the wasteland,
Bukcheong
His deep sigh also overpassed Hamkwanryeong and exiled to the
rough valley of the border.

함경도 북청 성동城東의 화피옥樺皮屋

무덤보다 못하지 않은가
자작나무 껍질 덧대어 지은 이 집에서
동지 이후 황달 들어 죽어가는데
꼿꼿이 일어서는 정신불이
온몸을 마구 헤집어
벌떡, 추사 몸 일어서다

* 화피옥 : 자작나무 껍질로 이어 붙여 지은 굴피집.

Bukcheong Sungdong Oak Bark Roof House

No better than a grave

In the house made of oak barks

Chusa, getting jaundice, was dying after the winter solstice

Just at that time spiritual fire standing upright

Shook the entire body to wake

Up sprangs Chusa.

함경감사 침계 윤정현

추사가 유배온 지 달포쯤 지나
삼십 년을 알고 지내는 제자, 침계가 함경감사로 부임하다
해배 후 추사가 사 년여 더 살 수 있었던 것은
추사를 극진히 공궤한 공이니, 침계여
조선 씨알들 깨어나 올리는 합장,
저승에서나마 서로 만나 포옹하시라

* 침계 : 윤정현의 호.

A Hamgyeong Governor, Yoon Jeonghyun

About a month after Chusa was exiled

His pupil Chimgye, going back 30 years, proceeded to his post as a
governor in Hamgyeongdo.

He might have lived 4 years longer

Thanks to Chimgye's devoted food offers.

The seeds of Joseon woke up and joined their hands in prayer.

May you meet together in heaven.

* Chimgye : Yoon Jeonghyun's pen name.

파발마

올 때는 번개처럼 달려오라
팔월 열사흘의 어명을 등줄기에 감고 달리는 말이여
석파 이하응이 보낸 빛이여

* 1852년(철종3) 추사 나이 67세 때의 8월 13일 해배 어명을 이하응이 알려오다.

A Post Horse

When you come, run to come like a thunder.
The horse, running with the royal command tied to its back.
You are a ray of light Seokpa Lee Haeung sent.

* On Auguest 13, 1852, Chusa was released from exile in Bukcheong.

자화煮火

탄생부터 손잡고 가까이에 동거하는 불길이
탱탱하게 부풀어 오르고 있다
검은 목소리가 이끄는 죽음의 덫에
초 녹여 물 먹인 실밥을 팔뚝에 세워놓는다
어려서 뗀 천자문, 자치통감이다
시, 서, 화, 금석학, 고증학, 경학, 실학, 불가의 정법들이
학예와 정치와 명상 그 번뇌의 불길 내어
불꽃 일생 살라 자신을 소멸시키는 살갗 태우며
팽팽하게 부풀어 타들어오고 있다

생의 근원을 깨워 고요의 평원에 닿는
추사 팔뚝의 심방에서 타는 불심지 정신인가

일흔한 살, 시공을 태우는 연비煙匪기도

The Prayer of Making a Burn on an Arm

The flame, born hand in hand and living together

Is growing up

By the death trap with dark voice.

On the forearm is put the thread, dipped into wax drippings.

Not only the Thousand-Character Classic and Zizhi Tongjian mastered in his childhood but also

Poetry, paintings and calligraphy, epigraphy, documental archaeology, Confucianism, Practical Learning, and Buddhist Rules

Build the fire of arts and sciences, politics, meditation, and earthly desires, and

Burn the flesh to forget oneself and live a flame life.

They are burning, swelling

Is the burning wick on the forearm Chusa's spirit

To wake the root of life up and reach the plain of tranquility?

71 years old. His prayer of making a burn to free from time and space,

추사, 영면하다

과지초당,
북청 유배객 추사가 해배되어
겨우겨우 귀향한 곳
선친 장례 후 삼년 간 시묘살이한 땅,
봉은사를 오가며
자화하다가
학예의 군주이자
일대의 통유 김정희,
하늘 시간 타고 영원 속으로
영면하다

* 추사가 봉은사 판전을 쓴 지 사흘 지난 1856년 10월 10일, 과지초당에서 영면하자 가
  족들은 지금의 예산군 신암면 용궁리 추사고택 옆에 장례를 모셨다.

Chusa, Rest in Peace

Gwajichodang,

A place Chusa returned to

After released from banishment, and

Where he mourned at the grave for 3 years after his father's funeral.

While coming and going to Bongeunsa, and

Receiving commandments of Buddhism,

The king of art and science and

The competent and executive scholar, Kim Jeonghui

Flew on the heavenly time into the eternal life.

In peace he rested.

붓의 폭발음

추사고택 마당귀에 뒹구는 흙 한 줌
백합이 구근 부풀리며 한 겨울철 땅 속의 검은 공기 마시는
평생이다, 평생 붓으로 숨 쉰 사내

한 평 유배지 방에서조차 붓에 들어가
천지간 음양의 이치와 천리天理의 오묘한 강줄기를 치고
허공에 뻗은 난초 잎을 친 사내가, 평생이다
한 평생 친 것은 붓의 자유, 그 하나다

천상에서 얻어온 천둥 혈맥 하나 키워
마침내 콸콸콸 쏟아져
메말라 가문 땅에 내리는 단비의 시원始原,

이런 것이다 심장을 찢는 붓의 폭발음!

Brush Blast

A handful of earth rolls in the yard, and
A lily breathes black air in to swell its bulb in the winter ground.
In his whole life, a man who's breathed through the brush.

In the brush even in the room of one pyeong
A man who's drawn orchids in the air. In his whole life, and
The profound principles of yin and yang and the nature.
What he's drawn in his life is only one, the freedom of the brush.

The thunder lineage from heaven grows and
At last, glug glug glug it rains
On the barren land, the origin of welcome rain.

That's it. The brush blast tearing the heart!